## She kne

Ben leaned ... "Talk to me ... ...g on your mind."

*He* was on her mind, but what she was thinking kept getting mixed up with what she was seeing—his physical presence. It dominated everything. He was wearing boots, well-washed jeans and a plaid shirt. He hadn't shaved, but he was the kind of man who looked good with a day's growth of beard. She wished she had a robe—a blanket—something to give her protection from his nearness. To distract herself, she turned to baby Amanda, nestled snugly in his strong arms.

"I should probably change the baby."

"Been done," Ben said calmly.

"Thanks," she said, still avoiding his glance. "You're better with Amanda than I." She couldn't believe how easily Ben handled the child—how content and calm Amanda seemed in his arms.

"Experience," he replied. "There's coffee," he added as he handed her a cup.

Their fingers touched in a gesture that made the morning seem intimate. A man and a woman sharing breakfast. A baby in his arms. The woman still in her nightclothes. Too intimate, she thought, for someone she knew nothing about.

## ABOUT THE AUTHOR

Shannon Harper and Madeline Porter have been published as Madeline Harper by Harlequin for over ten years. Many of their Temptation novels have appeared on the Waldenbooks and B. Dalton bestseller lists. Their partnership is unique, since Shannon lives on the East Coast and Madeline on the West, but with the help of faxes, phones and express mail, they've written over thirty books.

Shannon and Madeline love reading and writing mystery and suspense. And it goes without saying that they enjoy humor and romance. In *Baby in My Arms* they have tried to combine all those elements for a special book to celebrate the Christmas season. Happy holidays to all!

## Books by Madeline Harper

Don't miss any of our special offers. Write to us at the following address for information on our newest releases.

Harlequin Reader Service
U.S.: 3010 Walden Ave., P.O. Box 1325, Buffalo, NY 14269
Canadian: P.O. Box 609, Fort Erie, Ont. L2A 5X3

# Baby in My Arms
## Madeline Harper

## Harlequin Books

TORONTO • NEW YORK • LONDON
AMSTERDAM • PARIS • SYDNEY • HAMBURG
STOCKHOLM • ATHENS • TOKYO • MILAN
MADRID • WARSAW • BUDAPEST • AUCKLAND

To Bonnie Crisalli, for her advice,
enthusiasm and support.

ISBN 0-373-22400-1

BABY IN MY ARMS

Copyright © 1996 by Madeline Porter and Shannon Harper

## WESTERN UNITED STATES

# CAST OF CHARACTERS

**Kate McNair**—Becoming an instant mother wasn't on her agenda, but neither was being a gunman's target.

**Ben Blackeagle**—Reluctant bodyguard to Kate and her baby, he found himself deep in an unexpected mystery.

**Daniel Hedrick**—He was the lawyer who placed Kate's baby, but was he also in the baby black market?

**Kim Minter**—She was Hedrick's helpful assistant, but just how far *would* she go?

**Rudy Hall**—He was Kim's boyfriend—and more.

**Robert Brownley**—Head of one of Denver's most reputable charities, he had a dark secret.

**Jennifer Kersten**—Nothing happened at Sky High Spa without Jennifer's knowledge.

**Mark Kersten**—Jennifer's husband, he was bluff and brawny with more than a trace of menace in his eyes.

**Dylan**—He was the darling of the spa, always eager to help with a workout.

**Coral Lampiere**—Why had she sworn Kate to secrecy and then suddenly disappeared? And...

**Amanda**—Blond, blue-eyed and adorable—was this baby the reason that Kate's life was suddenly in danger?

# Chapter One

Kate took a wrong step, swore to herself and slipped on the ice. Regaining her balance, she came to a screeching halt.

"I'll never learn," she said aloud as she grabbed a parking meter and held on, surveying the sidewalk ahead. She hadn't noticed any patches of ice. But that was the problem; they were never obvious, especially in Denver. This was December weather unlike anything she'd ever known.

And that was under normal circumstances. Today, besides her briefcase and large handbag, there were a couple of unusual extras—the diaper bag over her shoulder and the year-old baby in a stroller beside her.

"No one's going to believe this," she said as the wind came up and whipped the scarf away from her face. She lowered her head and pointed herself and all her gear toward the office building ahead.

"Looks like you need some help, ma'am." A rotund Santa appeared beside her. "You and your baby."

"She's not my baby—" Kate began, and then shrugged as Santa held the door open wide.

She forged through it, muttering her thanks, and became enveloped in the warmth of the glorious indoors. But it was only moments before the comforting heat turned into an uncomfortable steamy blast. So far, this was what winter in Denver meant—wrap up to keep from freezing outside and then strip everything off inside to avoid roasting.

Kate peeled her way out of the scarf, coat and gloves. Then she crouched beside the baby.

"Hat's off," she said, untying Amanda's hood and pushing it back. She smoothed the soft golden curls from the little girl's face and took off her knitted cap. "When we get upstairs, Tina can help you out of that snowsuit." Otherwise known as a straitjacket, she added to herself.

Amanda made a swipe for her cap. Kate pulled it away but not quickly enough. The baby's grip was amazing. She looked up at Kate, bright blue eyes wide. "No?"

"No," Kate announced, then, "oh, well, why not?" She released the cap as she pushed the stroller into the elevator. "Might as well chew on that as some other things I can think of." Besides, if Amanda didn't have it she'd cry, and once she started crying, nothing could stop her.

The elevator was empty, and Kate gave a tired sigh as she leaned against the wall. Nothing in her twenty-six years had prepared her for instant motherhood.

The doors opened on the third floor, and Kate stumbled out, pushing the stroller ahead and dragging everything else behind—but, once again, not fast enough. The closing whoosh of the doors grabbed the diaper bag.

"Damn." She fought the bag out of the clutches of the elevator, kicking, cursing and pulling until she was victorious. Then she looked down to see that Amanda had dropped the cap and was staring at her, a look of pure surprise on her chubby pink face.

"What's the matter? Was it my curses? Well, stick around and you'll hear more," Kate said as she picked up the bonnet and pushed the stroller through the glass doors into the offices of Executive Search Services.

Her assistant, Tina Florio, looked up in amazement. "You brought the baby to *work?*"

"Please, Tina, I'm not in the mood for accusations—"

"It was just a comment," Tina assured her.

"Hmm," Kate replied. "Then let me explain this baby thing. First, the sitter didn't show, and I couldn't find her anywhere. Seems she decided to go away for the Christmas holidays without telling me. Next, I called five—yes, five—day-care centers. Not a one had openings. Then I called a nanny service. Shall I tell you what she said?"

"No openings?" Tina guessed.

"More emphatic—'ten days before Christmas— surely, you're not serious.' When I said I was perfectly serious, all I got was silence. She thought I was insane." Kate hung her ankle-length red coat in the closet.

"You know what, Tina?" She continued, answering her own question, "I believe I *am* insane—for taking on motherhood with no preparation. But I had no choice. Amanda was alone. She had no one." Kate blinked back tears. "I know she's terribly confused about all this."

"Kids her age are resilient," Tina assured her.

"I don't know about that, but she's certainly a little fighter—especially when it's time to dress. I spent nearly an hour trying to get her into all this paraphernalia—diapers, undershirt, that little embroidered blouse, the overalls, socks—and the shoes, which were impossible. She scrunched up her toes so I couldn't get the damned things on. As for the snowsuit—" Kate threw up her hands.

Tina's face wore the beginnings of a smile.

"Don't laugh," Kate warned. "You haven't heard anything yet. Have you ever tried to feed one of these—" She was momentarily speechless.

"Babies?" Tina offered.

"I'm only kidding. She's *some* baby, but every mealtime is a war. This morning she refused to open her mouth for the longest time. When I finally got food down her she smiled at me innocently and threw up on my blouse!"

Tina made a sound that was a near-laugh.

"Don't—" Kate said sternly.

"I won't," Tina promised, pressing her lips together. "That's the first thing they teach us at business school, not to laugh at our employers."

"Oh, sure," Kate said, "and you got an A, right?"

"You said it," Tina replied as she picked up Amanda. "Let me help. I have four younger sisters...." She extricated the baby from her snowsuit. "You're a little doll, Amanda. Look at those big blue eyes. Absolutely adorable."

The baby made a grab for Tina's shiny black hair, but Tina eluded her. "Forget the hair, kid." Tina looked up at Kate. "What are you going to do with her during your appointments?"

"I don't have any today," Kate answered. "This close to Christmas, no one's looking for managerial staff. They're too busy planning parties."

"All except for one."

Kate thought about taking off her boots and putting on heels, but she couldn't muster the energy. "What one?" she asked.

"The guy in your office."

"Be serious." There was no way she could handle appointments today, not after a night with Amanda. The baby had woken up at two in the morning, and Kate had tried every trick in the book to get her back to sleep. Failing that, and reminding herself that this baby was as traumatized as she, Kate had played with Amanda, invented games, walked her around the apartment, hoping she would tire. She didn't; Kate did.

"I *am* serious," Tina insisted. "The computer guy's in your office. The one ESS brought in to secure the system, remember? So rival placement services can't hack in and steal our client list. He's the one you stood up last week when you got hit by the car—"

"Oh, Lord," Kate moaned. "*That* guy. Just what I need, a computer nerd talking about bits and bytes and macros...."

"I'll be glad to deal with him," Tina offered, her brown eyes ingenuous.

"Umm. Well..."

Tina headed toward Kate's office.

"No," Kate decided. "I better handle it. Could you look after Amanda? There's a bottle somewhere in that bag. If she takes it, maybe she'll sleep for a while."

"It's only ten in the morning, Kate."

"She has day and night confused. She was up most of the night, so possibly she'll sleep...." Her voice drifted off, and Tina shrugged, a little unhappily, Kate thought. "Okay, I know this isn't in your job description—"

"I'll give it a try," Tina agreed. "Just promise you'll call me if you need any help with Mr. Blackeagle."

Again, Kate saw the glint in her secretary's eyes. "*Black* eagle? I thought it was just Eagle—Eagle Security."

"That's the company name. The man's a Native American. And what a native. You'll see."

NOT STOPPING to figure out Tina's cryptic remarks, Kate went into her office with the nerd image still in her mind—short, skinny and bespeckled.

The man at her computer terminal couldn't be the nerd, not with black denim pants hugging long legs, black leather jacket stretched across broad shoulders, and certainly not with ebony hair pulled back in a ponytail. But there was no one else in the room so the nerd was, in a word, the hunk. Ben Blackeagle.

"Mr. Blackeagle?" she asked.

He turned to look at her, and Kate tried not to stare. It was difficult. His eyes were dark and penetrating, like a bird's, but not friendly—more like a bird of prey. His nose was strong and aquiline, his cheekbones high and sculptured and his skin the color of pale copper. His chin was firm, squared and stubborn. She caught the gleam of a gold stud in his left ear.

What she couldn't take her eyes away from was his wide, sensuous mouth, which, as she watched, he drew into a tight, narrow line. "Ms. McNair? How nice of you to come to your office," he drawled. "I figured you for a no-show again."

Kate decided to ignore the rude remark. After all, he had a point, which she didn't feel like getting into. She offered a friendly smile and her hand.

"Kate McNair. Sorry about being late today. As for our first appointment . . ." She decided to let that one go. He could finish it however he chose.

He didn't respond but took her hand with a grasp that was brief but powerful. She had just enough time to notice that his hands were strong and sinewy, with long lean fingers.

He dropped her hand and looked at her with his almost black eyes. They fixed on hers. "Our first appointment," he repeated. And then he waited, expectantly.

"Well . . ." She was usually sure of herself, able to talk with anyone, never intimidated. What was happening here?

He didn't shift his gaze. It demanded a response.

*But wait a minute,* she thought. *I'm employing him, not the other way around. I don't owe this guy an explanation.* Then, suddenly, she was explaining. "Ten days ago, I was on my way to the office, and I got hit by a car—"

He looked at her skeptically. "You recovered quickly. Nothing serious, I see."

"Maybe not serious in medical terms, but it's all relative, and I was very badly bruised and shaken," she said defensively. "I was taken to the emergency room and later sent home. It took me several days to recover. Then the baby came—"

"Wait a minute. You had a baby—at home—just days after being hit by a car?"

She laughed. "No, no. I—well, I kind of inherited the baby, my cousin's daughter. Libby—and her husband, Derek—are, that is, they were—the baby's parents. They were in a commuter plane crash...." She swallowed hard.

He was silent, politely quiet and serious.

"They were both killed." It was still difficult for her to talk about.

"Sorry," he muttered.

She nodded. "As the closest relative, I kind of inherited the baby and we're both trying to adjust." As she completed her explanation, she crossed the room, assuming a more businesslike demeanor, wishing she'd changed into her other shoes.

Ben leaned back against the computer table and crossed one ankle over the other, eyeing his potential employer. Kate McNair, manager of Executive Search Services, was like many of the career women he'd met. Nothing about her was unusual or unexpected. Her brown suit was well tailored and severe, her blouse cream-colored and understated. Like her office, she was neat and professional.

But something was different, Ben thought. It could be the red hair. It wasn't the expected strawberry-blond red, but red-red. He thought of the flames of a plains fire, whipping up against the harsh white snow.

There wasn't another red quite like that, and he'd *never* seen it in a woman's hair.

A few wisps of that fiery hair slipped away from her French twist, and there was something—it looked like a stain—on the lapel of her dress-for-success blouse. This young executive on the way up, he mused, somehow missed the mark and became a real person.

Ben considered himself an expert in two areas—computers and women. In both cases, he knew when they were accessible to him and when they weren't. Kate McNair was not his type, although the statistics seemed right: about five feet six inches, slender, small nose, full sensual lips, green eyes. But something didn't work. He could see it in the tired look in her eyes. Parenthood could do that to a person. She was attractive, he decided, but a career woman with a baby was definitely not for him.

"I've never known anyone who inherited a kid," he remarked.

"Neither have I, actually," she said, adding, with a sigh, "I'm as surprised as anyone. I didn't expect—" She caught herself. "But we're not here to talk about babies."

"You're right about that, Ms. McNair." His voice was cool, uninvolved.

"Call me Kate, please."

"Sure, Kate. I'm Ben. Your home office, back in New York, wants this computer system to be hacker-proofed. Have you experienced any problems?" he asked in a voice that she found suddenly brusque.

"Not yet, but I've only been in the Denver office about six weeks." She dropped her briefcase on the desk and turned back toward him.

Ben's six-foot-two-inch frame and broad shoulders seemed to fill the room. It was too early in the morning to be faced with someone so...so overwhelmingly male. Even though she hated to admit it, Kate thought, he was incredibly sexy.

What was it? Easy, she told herself, it was the great body, the dark hungry eyes, the husky, growling voice. No wonder Tina had wanted to get into the office with him!

Kate tripped the latch of her briefcase, opened it and looked at him over the raised black leather top. "I hear that some of the other offices have been raided by rival placement services. They hack in and steal client lists—"

"Applicants looking for jobs?"

"No, they usually hit the corporate lists, the companies that hire staff through ESS," she told him.

He turned back to the computer, his fingers moving quickly over the keyboard. In less than a minute, a list of ESS corporate clients appeared on the screen.

"How'd you do that?" she asked.

"If I told you, then you wouldn't need my services." He grinned. "The fact is, your system is much too easy to crack even without your password. But in this case, I had the word."

"Who told you?"

"No one. I guessed. On the third try—DOS."

"How—"

"You'd be surprised how many people use computer terms like mac, doc, dir—and DOS."

"Well, it was so easy to remember, I thought..."
Her voice drifted off.

"Don't worry. Just about any three-letter password can be broken. Besides, that's not the only way for hackers to get in. I'll block access wherever possible, but first, I'll set you up with a five-letter password that'll be more difficult to access."

"Don't make it some crazy combination of consonants that I won't be able to remember," she asked.

"That's the problem with you people. You take this so lightly."

"'You people' isn't really me. I'm not a computer type," she explained. "That's Tina's area. I guess I'm not what you call 'computer friendly.'"

"But you do *use* the computer?"

"Yes, sometimes, but—"

"Then you need to become 'friendly,'" he insisted.

Kate silently fumed. She'd had an awful night. Night? She'd had a horrible ten days. Now some computer jock was lecturing her. Through gritted teeth, she asked, "What can I do to help you get started?"

"Have breakfast with me."

"I'm sorry?" She wasn't going to be put on.

"Let's have breakfast," he insisted.

He'd gotten on her case for missing one appointment, being late for another and not being computer friendly. Now he wanted to have breakfast with her! "I can't do that. I've missed too much work. First there was the accident. Then Amanda arrived...." She was repeating herself. And besides, why did she think she had to explain to the man hired to solve a few computer problems? She added pointedly, "We can send out for coffee."

"But I want more than coffee. I want a real breakfast. Eggs. Hash browns. Biscuits. I was out late last night—on a special project." A sly smile played around his lips.

Sure, she thought. There was no way his special project had anything to do with computers. "I don't have time," she said stubbornly.

"Look, I'm going to breakfast. If you come with me, we can get all the talk about the system over with. Then we can both go back to work. You do your thing. I do my thing, and I'm outta here by five o'clock, my job over and done."

"No, I—"

"Suit yourself. It's up to you." He spoke in a voice that was pleasant but firm.

Kate sighed. Ben Blackeagle was obviously going to do things his way or no way. She was too tired to argue. What did an hour more or less mean in a life that was totally out of control anyway? Besides, she was hungry, too.

"I suppose I could bring the baby—"

"The baby's here?"

She nodded. "Maybe Tina will watch her."

Ben raised a skeptical eyebrow. "Your secretary doesn't look like the baby-sitter type."

Kate couldn't help laughing. He was right about that. With her long legs, high boots, short skirts, moussed hair, perfect features augmented by fabulous makeup, Tina had her own agenda. Baby-sitting didn't figure in it. In fact, ESS was only a stopping-off place on her way to a modeling career.

But she had all those little sisters, Kate remembered. "I'll ask," she decided.

Abruptly she went through the door into the outer office where Tina appeared to be huddled over her computer; in fact, she was huddled over Amanda. She looked up, her finger with its salon-manicured fingernail touching her lips.

"Sssh," she whispered. She'd lowered the back of the stroller, and Amanda was sleeping. "She's beat."

"Who isn't?" Kate asked. She followed up quickly with another question. "Since she's down-and-out, would you watch her while I have breakfast with Mr. Blackeagle?"

Tina raised a perfectly sculptured eyebrow.

"He's hungry." Getting no sympathetic response, she added, "And my best bet is to work with him over breakfast."

"Understood," Tina said.

"Then you'll watch the baby?"

"Of course. I'm not going anywhere," Tina replied. "But bring me back coffee and a Danish."

"You've got it," Kate said. "And it's my treat." She reached for her coat on the wall hook, and suddenly Ben was there, holding it for her.

"Well, Little Red Riding Hood, met any wolves recently?" he asked.

Kate glanced quickly at Tina and saw her secretary hide a grin.

"I'm not crazy about red," she admitted. "But when I was ready to transfer here from Phoenix, I had to put together a new wardrobe. This was the only coat I could find that was heavy enough for Denver."

He looked at her speculatively.

"This color wouldn't have been my first choice," she added. Why was she so defensive? Because Ben seemed to know how to push all the right buttons.

He chuckled. "You should be warm enough," he said easily. The long red coat covered her from neck to ankles. He knew what was underneath, and it was a totally business look, but he could always imagine something more interesting.

"We'll be back soon," Kate assured, ignoring Ben's remark—and his wry look.

At the elevator, Ben pushed the button and commented, "Cute kid."

That made Kate relax a little as she agreed, "I think so, too, but she's really active, like any one-year-old, I guess." The elevator doors slid open and they stepped in. "She's learning to walk, and she's ready to practice anytime—especially in the middle of the night."

"Hmm," he agreed. "Actually, I was talking about your secretary."

"Calling her a cute kid?" Kate asked, aghast.

Ben laughed.

"You're not serious?"

"Of course not," he replied.

She walked along beside him, willing to believe that he was joking, but not quite sure. Ben Blackeagle was definitely an enigma. His next remark added to the confusion.

"Amanda is obviously your first child. Otherwise you'd know they don't run on schedules like an office."

Kate looked sideways at him. Was he speaking from experience? She wasn't about to ask whether he had a wife—or children—of his own.

"I saw a restaurant on the corner," he told her as they left the building. "You want to go there?"

"Sure," she said. "That's as good a choice as any."

They walked along the slushy street, Kate hurrying to match his long strides. By the time they reached the corner, she looked around nervously. Since the accident, she'd been anxious, especially at intersections. But with Ben beside her, she felt more secure.

Besides, there were no pedestrians except her and Ben and only a few cars at the crossing. He offered his arm and she took it. They stepped off the curb into the street.

That was when she heard the loud, cracking sound, like a car backfiring. But different. Closer. Louder.

Then Ben yelled, "Get down. Now!"

She felt the weight of his body falling on her, knocking her back onto the sidewalk as another shot rang out.


TWO POLICEMEN answered the call—a young man, eager and alert, and an older woman, bored and laconic. By the time they arrived, Ben was settled in the coffee shop, finishing up a plate of fried eggs, hash browns, sausage, bacon and toast. Huddled over a cup of coffee, Kate glowered at him. They'd been shot at, and he was feeding his face, acting as if nothing had happened.

The young officer recapped information he'd gathered, reading from notes. "No one in the coffee shop, the newsstand or the office across the street saw anything—no shooter, not even a suspicious-looking character. There's not a single witness."

His partner lit a cigarette, ignoring the No Smoking signs strategically placed on the tables. "Drive-by shooting," she said.

Ben finished his eggs and wiped his mouth without comment.

Kate couldn't believe his nonchalance, especially when she was so involved. "In this part of town? I haven't lived in Denver very long, but this doesn't seem like gang territory to me."

The young officer responded. "It's not, but the lines are beginning to blur, unfortunately. If they want to leave their turf, nothing's stopping them."

"But why would they shoot at us?" she asked.

"We don't even know that's what happened. But if it is, you two were just in the wrong place at the wrong time."

Kate's hand shook as she picked up her cup. The coffee was bitter—and cold. Grimacing, she put it down. "Seems to be happening to me a lot recently—being in the wrong place."

The young officer leaned forward. "What do you mean by that, ma'am?"

"About ten days ago, I was on First Avenue in Cherry Creek, waiting for a light to change. The sidewalk was crowded with shoppers, and I was jostled, pushed in front of a car."

Ben looked up, suddenly curious.

"You think there's a connection between that incident and this one?" the officer wondered.

"I imagine there's an easy explanation," the policewoman commented. "Your boots."

"My boots?" Kate asked.

"Yes. High heels with leather soles."

Kate felt three pairs of eyes riveted to her boots. She pulled her feet under the table.

"They're no good on ice. You should think about getting some real boots with traction. You probably just slipped," the woman continued.

"Did you file a police report, Ms. McNair?" the young man asked.

She shook her head. "No one saw anything so I could only assume that it was an accident."

He studied his notes. "And both of you deny having any enemies."

Kate frowned. *Deny having enemies.* That made them seem at fault. "None," she said firmly.

"Same for me," Ben replied, speaking up for the first time—now that breakfast was over. "All my customers are satisfied."

"You two known each other long?" the woman asked.

"We met this morning over business," Kate replied. "There's no connection between us at all. No one could possibly know we were going to be together today," she added firmly.

The woman stood up. "That covers all the bases. Come on, Riley, we got to get moving."

"That's it?" Kate asked indignantly.

"We'll make a report, ma'am," the young officer explained politely. "But it doesn't look like the shooter was aiming at you or Mr. Blackeagle. We found one of the bullets...."

"Ballistics!" Kate exclaimed. "You can trace it."

The policewoman shook her head. "All we can get is the make of the gun. I can tell you now it was probably a rifle."

"Well, then—" Kate began.

"This is Colorado, Ms. McNair."

Kate looked at her, frowning.

The young officer clarified his partner's remark. "Lots of folks own rifles out here."

The woman was more impatient. "You and Mr. Blackeagle both deny having enemies. There've been no threats. All we can do is wait. If there's another attempt—"

Kate moaned.

"More than likely it's an isolated event," Riley added. "Things like this happen frequently, I'm sorry to say." He settled his cap firmly on his head. "You have our names and the precinct's phone number. Call if we can help—or if you think of anything else."

Kate watched their retreating backs. "I can't believe it. They're not going to do anything!"

Ben pushed his empty plate away and waved the waitress over for a refill of his coffee. "They checked for witnesses. They asked questions. No one saw anything. We don't know who—or what—the target was. Probably some guy, high on drugs or booze, celebrating Christmas early with a little random shooting. As the officer said, things like that happen, Kate."

She sighed. "I guess you're right, but I can't take much more excitement." She shook her head in wonder. Her life seemed totally out of control, but she tried not to think of that as she managed a tremulous smile. "Thanks, Ben. If you hadn't knocked me down, I'd be dead."

"No, I don't think—"

"Yes, it's true. I could have been hit by the second shot. Except for you."

"It was just reflex," he replied. "Hope I didn't hurt you."

"Nope. Just my coat."

"I hurt your coat?"

She laughed. "No, you didn't *hurt* it. You just sort of—mangled it." Her red coat was lying across a chair, a wide grease smear along the hem, the back soaked with melted snow. She lowered her eyes, remembering how he'd treated her coat—and her, recalling the feeling of his body on hers.

As scared as she'd been when the gunshot sounded, her heart pumping like a runaway engine, she'd still been very aware of him, all hard muscles, shielding her from danger. She raised her eyes to his. They were dark and fathomless.

"After everything that's happened—getting caught in gunfire, especially—I realize you got more than you bargained for, and I wouldn't blame you if you called it quits with ESS and canceled the contract," Kate told him.

"No way. My word is my bond. That's what makes my company successful."

"Of course," she said. "And I'm sure you *are* successful."

"When I finish up with ESS, I'll take a few days off and then I'm heading for Christmas vacation in Puerto Vallarta and some heavy-duty partying," he replied, in answer to her comment. "Meanwhile, I'm here in Denver being shot at." He cocked a dark eyebrow. "This is kinda farfetched, but could some of your rivals in the job placement business be jealous enough to take a shot at you?"

She shook her head. "What would that accomplish? ESS would just hire someone to replace me. I haven't been here long enough for them to care. And I certainly haven't been here long enough to make any friends—or enemies. So that leaves you. Friends? Enemies?"

"Lots of friends, no enemies." He finished his coffee and stood up, holding Kate's coat for her.

"We never got around to talking about securing the system," she reminded him.

"Don't worry, it's not going to be a problem."

She reached for the bill, but he stopped her. "My treat. And as for your system, I'll figure it out—before the day is over," he promised.

"Which reminds me, it's nearly noon now, and Tina must be frantic."

They stepped out into the cold hard glare of the December day. She stopped, hesitant, until Ben took her elbow and hustled her across the street. Even though he carried on a normal conversation, talking about the computer program, making suggestions, asking questions, the whole time he was watching, wary. There was protection in his big frame and tough-looking leather-clad exterior. His dark clothes, his size, his sense of assurance, all of these worked together to make him a formidable presence.

Once they were inside her office building and on the elevator, she breathed easier, but she couldn't relax completely. She'd been shot at in broad daylight on her way to breakfast. It didn't seem possible. It was like a dream. Or, actually a nightmare!

She shivered despite her warm coat and the heat of the elevator. She didn't like the way her life was going these days—a seemingly uncontrolled slide into chaos. Somehow she had to put the shooting incident behind her and concentrate on her work. The work was the important thing. If she didn't start producing, the ESS headquarters might regret making her their newest manager. Then she would be out of a job.

She was dedicated, hardworking, on the right track for her career. The problem was, improbable situations kept throwing her off track.

They stepped off the elevator and were met by Tina and Amanda.

One normal-size woman and one little baby, they seemed to take up the entire hall. It was the energy, Kate realized as she watched the two of them, Amanda stumping along on her short, chubby legs, arms over her head, hands held firmly by Tina, who was making some sort of chirping noises, whether to mollify the baby or herself, Kate couldn't be sure.

"The phone woke her," Tina explained over her shoulder to Kate as they sailed past.

"I'm sorry, we—" Kate attempted.

"Then she cried, and then she walked, then she cried *and* walked. God, it took you long enough. And where's my Danish?"

"I forgot, we had a problem—"

Tina seemed to focus in on her boss. "What happened? Were you hit by another car? Look at your coat!"

Before Kate could explain, Amanda surged forward, pulling Tina along.

"Ma-ma," she said chirpily. Then she caught sight of Ben and broke into a huge smile.

"Da-da, Da-da!"

## Chapter Two

Ben wasn't eavesdropping. He didn't care anything about Kate's pitch to potential clients. But what could he do in the confines of her small office, separated from her by no more than a body length? Without really listening, he absorbed the thrust of her conversations.

And he had to hand it to her, Kate McNair's style was a double-whammy; she was resilient *and* persistent. The shooting episode had definitely frightened her, but she didn't let it stand in the way of business as usual. And she didn't take no for an answer.

He listened as she got personnel managers on the phone and extolled the virtues of her placement service, not hanging up until she had an appointment. They were all scheduled for after the new year, though; no matter how persistent, she couldn't fight the holidays. Apparently, Christmas was a lousy time for job placement.

They'd had lunch—sandwiches ordered from the local deli—and Kate had taken a couple of long breaks to relieve Tina and bond with the baby. Only her quality time didn't seem very effective. Through the closed office door, he'd heard Kate's voice as she struggled to amuse the baby. The last effort, which included a bout of baby giggles and another of tears, was followed by silence. Nap time had evidently arrived, allowing Kate to return to her office and her phone.

"Coral Lampiere, please." Hearing only one side of the conversation, Ben easily imagined the other, which was obviously frustrating to Kate. She doodled on a pad as she listened, frowning.

"So you have no idea when she'll return? She didn't tell you—" Interrupted, Kate pushed away a lock of red hair from her eyes and tried again. "It just seems strange that there's no information—" Once again, she stopped midsentence. "Okay, I see. Thanks."

She hung up the phone and glared at it. "Happy holidays to you, too, you—" She stopped herself and looked up at Ben. "I'm usually not this volatile." She laughed. "That's what I told Amanda when her diaper bag got caught in the elevator! What a day. What a week. What a—" She stopped herself again. "You don't want to hear."

Ben looked up from the computer screen with a smile. "I think I get the point. Christmas is playing havoc with your business."

"Not to mention my life." She sighed. "Which impacts on my business."

There seemed to be a sense of humor hidden behind her problems, he thought.

"I thought this last call would lead to an easy appointment. It was a sure thing. Carol, who now calls herself Coral—is an old friend, or at least an acquaintance. She owns Sky-High Spa, and she made a verbal commitment to me to restaff through ESS. She wanted to hire immediately, and now she's gone. Out of town. Just like Amanda's baby-sitter—they're leaving me in droves!''

''I'm sure it has nothing to do with you personally.''

''Lord, I hope not. But I really hate missing that spa job. The place is a very popular spot, or so I hear. Do you belong to a workout club?''

''Me?'' Ben laughed. ''No, I'm not into aerobics. Don't have a leotard,'' he added with a grin.

''I suppose there're plenty of gyms in Denver where men can wear sweats,'' she retorted. ''Sky-High Spa is for women, but I haven't even been inside yet.''

''She's your old friend—''

''Acquaintance,'' Kate corrected.

''And you've never been to the spa that you're staffing for her?''

''I closed the deal over lunch—or thought I did. So much for friendship.''

''And for workout spas,'' he said as he leaned back, his long legs stretched in front of him. He'd taken off the leather jacket, slung it over a chair and rolled up the sleeves of his dark flannel shirt. As if drawn by a magnet, her eyes focused on his forearms—sleek, smooth and muscular. Not satisfied with that view, she slid her gaze up to his shoulders and then to the sturdy column of his neck. It was obvious that Ben Blackeagle was in great shape.

''I bet you work out, though,'' she persisted. God, what was the matter with her, prying into his life and asking about his exercises? She sounded like a teenager with overactive hormones.

''I'm a runner of sorts.''

She knew it!

''And I lift weights at home sometimes.''

Kate smiled in satisfaction, particularly pleased that he didn't seem irritated with her nosiness.

But the conversation was at a standstill, and she couldn't think of anything else to say. The room seemed very small, and Ben was very large. And close to her. She could see the slow, rhythmic movement of his chest as he breathed in and out. The afternoon sun gleamed on his black hair and coppery skin. He regarded her with one eyebrow raised, waiting for her to go on.

She couldn't. Something inside of her was going crazy, and Kate was having real trouble controlling it. What could she possibly be thinking, letting her imagination go so wild? She decided to stop the feelings before they got out of hand.

"Tina," she called, getting up and walking to the office door.

As she disappeared, Ben watched, amused. A woman of impulse, he decided, who was definitely flustered. He let his mind dwell on her as she went through the door—the look of her, the shape of her. Damned good on both counts.

When she returned, she was businesslike. Whatever he thought he'd seen in her look must have been imagined, Ben decided.

"How's it going?" she asked casually.

"Almost done."

She sat behind her desk. "I have a feeling we made a good choice with Eagle Security. Is yours a family business?"

"Hardly. I grew up on the reservation. No superhighway there."

"What kind of Indian—I mean Native American—are you?" She stumbled a little but recovered. "That is, what tribe, if it's not a rude question."

"Not at all. I get asked all the time, and I'm proud to answer. My father was Arapaho, my mother Cheyenne and Irish."

"That's so—exotic," she said, feeling a little ridiculous. But she'd never met anyone of Native American heritage. "Cheyenne and Arapaho..."

"You left out the Irish part. Don't you think that's exotic?"

"Well, yes, but—"

"Just kidding, Kate." He looked at her with amusement in his dark eyes. "Now, if you have the time, I'll show you how I've protected the computer system, the new way to log on and off and a few other changes. You might want to write some of this down."

"All of it," she said. "Remember, I'm not any good at computer stuff—"

"*Yet,*" he finished for her. "Soon you will be. Now sit here and let me show you what I've done."

As instructed, she sat at the terminal with Ben standing behind her, teacher and student. Yet it was much more than that. This was no classroom, and Ben Blackeagle was not an ordinary teacher. Not ordinary at all.

As he leaned forward, his chest grazed her hair. She was very aware of him, so much so that she found it hard to concentrate on the screen and kept making mistakes.

"Damn, how did I get back to the menu?" she asked, turning to look at him. "I meant to go to the next page," she added, trying to catch her breath. She never should have turned around, not in these close quarters. She warned herself to keep looking straight at the screen, mistake or no mistake.

"You hit F2 instead of F10."

"Oh, that's right. Now I—"

"F10 again," he told her. "Remember?"

"Yes, I've got it," she said. But she didn't "get it" at all; she was going nowhere. But each time she messed up, he was there to correct her, often moving her hand away and showing her the keys to strike with his long, lean fingers, urging her to make notes.

She did. In a feeble handwriting, telling herself that the tenseness she felt was the result of the peril they'd experienced just a few hours before. Didn't sharing a common danger heighten feelings between two people, bind them in some way?

She made another mistake and the screen went blank. "I've lost everything," she said, willing herself not to turn around and look at him but to concentrate on the screen—blank though it was—instead. She sat silently, feeling the warmth of his breath on her neck.

"Remember the command?"

She looked at her notes. "Control Q?"

"Right," he said encouragingly.

She tried the combination. Nothing happened. "Major mistake this time," she said.

"It's my fault. I wasn't paying attention," he added. Which was the truth. He'd been watching but not concentrating, mesmerized instead by the scent of her, a faint whiff of an unidentifiable perfume. It filled his nostrils and was damned disconcerting. Add to that the graceful movement of her wrists, the faint click of her nails on the keys and that crazy red hair. A few shiny strands had come loose from her chignon and curled against the creamy skin of her neck as she bent forward over the keyboard. It was a very nice neck, Ben mused. Pale and silky looking.

For one rash and improbable moment he wondered what would happen if he bent down and kissed it, ran his tongue lightly across the soft skin. Then he smiled wryly. Not enough sleep and too much excitement during the morning must have gotten to him.

He pushed aside his fantasy with a sharp reprimand to remember his rule: never mix business with the pursuit of women. Those were very separate, although both important, components of his life.

During his reverie, he'd automatically corrected her mistake and returned the document to the screen. She was working away on it, doing better, according to her exclamations.

"I'm getting, it, Ben. Look, I saved, sent the document to the printer and exited—the right way." She turned toward him and flashed a proud smile.

The smile lit her eyes and brightened her face. She was pleased with herself, and the look of satisfaction was appealing and beguiling to him. He returned the smile and came damned close to giving her a congratulatory hug, which was definitely not part of the agenda.

Instead, he straightened up, reminding himself that he wasn't going to get involved. "Keep on working," he said, a shade too brusquely. "I'll go out and get Tina caught up on the changes. Shouldn't take long."

She turned back to the keyboard. What had passed between them in that momentary flash when she looked back at him? Nothing but her imagination, Kate told herself. Or maybe he'd seen something in her eyes, an invitation that he'd reacted against. She never should have turned around again. It had made her too vulnerable.

KATE WAS ON A ROLL, concentrating mightily and achieving all the goals Ben had set up for her without thinking about him at all. Except a few times. She went straight through until five o'clock, when Tina appeared in the doorway with Amanda in her arms.

"I'm checking out, Kate. Ben's finished with me. He's taking care of a few glitches. And, as you can see, our baby's awake."

"Okay, I'm done here, too. Thanks for your help, Tina." She exited the computer and got up. "Maybe tomorrow will be easier," she said hopefully, taking Amanda from Tina's arms.

"Got a baby-sitter yet?"

"Nope, but I'll make some more calls before I leave the office. Any ideas?"

"Not a one. And don't look at me."

"Of course not. You and I both have to work. But what about your sisters?"

"Two in school, two working. Sorry."

"Don't worry, I'll find someone."

"I hope so." Tina headed for the door and then turned back for a parting shot. "In case you haven't noticed, the baby's wet."

"I noticed. See you tomorrow." Holding Amanda at arm's length, she grabbed the diaper bag from behind Tina's desk—where Ben was bent over the terminal—and headed for the rest room.

"Ready to leave?" he asked.

"Nope. Just changing the baby. I plan to be around for another hour or so."

"Good," he called after her. "That'll give me time to run through these programs again before I shut down for the night."

"I'll be right back," Kate told him.

She was glad he'd be staying. Even though it was just after five o'clock, an early-winter darkness had fallen, and Kate didn't like the feeling of being alone. She hurried down the hall into the rest room, where she changed Amanda with the usual amount of awkwardness.

At least she'd discovered disposable diapers with self-adhesive tabs and no longer poked herself—or Amanda—with safety pins. But she still had problems. Amanda kicked and bucked and squirmed more than usual, and Kate had to hold on to keep her from falling off the narrow ledge between the sink and the paper towel dispenser that served as a changing counter.

"It's not ideal, I know, Amanda. But it has to do for now, so be a good girl and stop kicking."

As usual, the advice had no effect. "I admit I'm no good at this motherhood bit so you have to be patient with me, and I'll do the same for you—or try to." Amanda blew her bangs out of her eyes as she leaned over, attempting to fasten the snaps on Amanda's overalls. "Someone should invent another solution to this, maybe an outside zipper. Hey, that's not a bad idea."

Amanda looked up at her with a pout that turned to a smile and Kate planted a kiss on her fat pink cheek. "I know it's tough on you, too. Poor baby, you deserve a better mom."

"Ma-ma," Amanda responded.

Kate shook her head as she picked up the baby and went back down the hall toward her office. The elevators were quiet. Everyone had left on time—for parties or shopping, she imagined. Or a nice cozy dinner.

Dinner! She had nothing at home to eat, not even a jar of baby food. "Sorry, Amanda," she murmured. "We'll have to stop by the grocery store on the way home." She couldn't seem to get it together—diapers, bottles, baby food, baby-sitters....

Ben had shut down Tina's system and was in Kate's office, his eyes fixed on the computer screen.

"Finding any problems?"

"Nope. You're secure. But this billing program's a mess. Who set it up?"

"I have no idea," she replied.

"There're lots of easier ways to do it."

"I don't suppose you'd consider—"

"Nope. Security only. But I can suggest a couple of people—and there's an excellent manual—"

Kate shook her head. "Human beings work better for me."

"Well, this human's all finished here."

"You're ready to leave?" She tried to keep panic out of her voice.

"Unless you have some other problems...."

"None that I know of."

"I don't anticipate any in the future." He unwound himself from the chair. "Because I do good work," he added with a lazy smile that was full of assurance.

Kate made a quick decision. "Then let's close up. I can make my other calls from home tonight." She'd suddenly realized that she didn't want to be left alone in the building. "Now where'd I put that snowsuit?" As she looked around, the baby squirmed in her arms with the backward jackknife that she seemed so fond of. "I wish she wouldn't do that. She's strong for her size, and one of these days she's going to bolt right out of my arms."

"Babies know how to dominate and take advantage," Ben agreed, holding out his arms to the baby.

He hadn't meant to do that. He'd meant to put on his jacket and leave, but Kate seemed so awkward and inept around the kid, something made him reach out. "Come here, Mandy. I'll hold you while your mother—uh, Kate, gets your snowsuit."

"Da-da," Amanda gurgled. "Da-da-da-da."

"Not on your life," he said with a laugh, taking the baby expertly in his grasp and then tossing her into the air.

Amanda laughed hysterically and let out another stream of da-das. With the baby occupied, Kate made a dash for the outer office and came back with the snowsuit. She dreaded trying to stick pudgy little legs that went as soft as cooked spaghetti into the pant legs. Maybe Ben would attempt it for her, she thought. If he was as good at clothing them as he was at playing with them. . . .

She wondered where he got the skills. Somehow, she couldn't imagine a wife and kids, not for a guy who stayed out all night on "special projects." But you never knew.

He'd positioned Amanda on his ankle and was playing some kind of horsey game, holding her hands and bouncing her on his foot. Amanda gurgled with delight. Kate leaned against the door, watching and wondering again how he knew so much about children. There was no point in asking; she'd never see him again. But she was curious.

"Toss me the snowsuit," he ordered. "I can get her into it."

With relief, Kate complied and stood by as he cajoled Amanda into the suit in what she considered record time. He was too good; she *had* to ask. "How come it's so easy for you?"

"Lots of practice with younger brothers and sisters. But don't look at me," he added quickly. "My child-care days are over."

Kate shook her head. "Why do you and Tina both think I'm trying to rope you into baby-sitting?"

"Can't imagine." He pulled up the hood of Amanda's snowsuit and looked up at Kate with a glint in his eye.

"Well, I'm not. Tonight I'm getting on the phone and finding a suitable person for the job." She gathered her take-home work, baby-sitter and child-care lists and stuffed everything into her briefcase.

He pulled on his jacket. "I'll walk you ladies to your car. Night comes quickly in winter."

"I'd appreciate that." The dark outside was thick and unwelcoming, and she was glad to have company at least as far as her car. She slipped on her coat and picked up Amanda's diaper bag and scattered toys. Finally ready, she held out her arms for the baby. "I can put her into the stroller," she offered.

Amanda's mouth closed in a tight little circle, lower lip stuck out. "No," she said, clutching at Ben's collar.

"I'd better carry her," he said. "It'll make things simpler."

Kate turned out the light and locked the office door. *Simpler?* Would her life ever be simple again?

The air outside hit them like an icy knife. Kate tied Amanda's hood securely and pulled up the collar of her coat. "Aren't you cold?" she asked Ben, who was bareheaded and gloveless.

"Yep, but you know us stoical red men. We don't complain."

Kate thought he was teasing her but couldn't be sure. He wasn't just stoical; he was quixotic, unreadable. She knew practically nothing about Ben Blackeagle—and that was the way it would have to stay. Once she and Amanda drove away, that would be the end of her brief, but interesting—even frightening— day with him. At least she could be glad that he'd been there during the shooting, as her protector. Unless of course the attacker had been after *him*. She supposed they would never know the answer to that.

They trudged along, in the opposite direction from the shooting site, and Kate realized that while she should feel safe, she didn't, even with Ben beside her. She glanced up at him. He seemed wary, too. There was something stealthy about the way he moved, silent, careful.

Maybe she was thinking of a scene from a movie— the handsome Native American, his eyes steely as he surveyed the horizon, the sudden movement in the bush. He lifted his bow, pulled back, the muscles in his arms straining, and let the arrow fly. She could almost smell the excitement of the hunt.

"Where's your car?" he asked.

"Car?" She was having trouble getting back to reality. "Oh, there, across the street."

"Good. I'm parked there, too." Only half a dozen cars remained in the parking lot.

"That's mine, under the light." Kate pointed out a beige compact.

As they neared the car, Ben stopped. "You won't be going anywhere in this tonight."

"What—"

"Look at the tires."

"Oh, my God." Kate let out a cry. Both back tires were flat.

Ben handed the baby to her and walked around to the front of the car. She watched, her mind spinning as she tried to figure out what could have happened. The car had been serviced recently. The tires weren't new, but they were in good shape.

"The front tires are flat, too," Ben said.

She sagged against the car. "How could this have happened? I drove straight here from home. There was nothing unusual, no construction, no nails..."

Ben straightened and came toward her. "This wasn't an accident. Someone punctured all the tires." He stared at her intently. "What the hell is going on, Kate?"

She was shivering uncontrollably from a mixture of cold, anger—and fear. "I don't know."

Ben's face was serious, and there was a hint of suspicion in his voice. "You don't *know?* First you're hit by a car, then you're shot at—"

"We can't be sure the shots were for me. The police said it was probably a random shooting, a drive-by or whatever they call it. Or someone could have been shooting at you—"

"But they slashed *your* tires," he reminded her. "Looks like someone wanted you stranded here. Vulnerable.'' He looked around quickly. ''Whoever did this could be watching now. My Bronco's over there. Get in it.''

''Where are we going?''

''Away from here,'' he said.

''But I need to call road service, get the tires—''

''That can wait until tomorrow. Right now, we're getting out of here.''

He was right. They didn't need to stand in the middle of a deserted parking lot, arguing. She took a step toward his car. Then she remembered. ''Amanda's car seat—''

''Give me your keys.''

She did as she was told. He pulled out his key ring, found his car key and pressed it in her hand. ''Go,'' he urged and she took off at a sprint, Amanda bobbling in her arms, chortling with delight at the unexpected motion.

With shaky hands, Kate unlocked the car and crawled in. Moments later, Ben was on the other side. ''Unlock the door,'' he called out.

''Amanda's seat goes in the back—''

''I know.'' He settled the car seat and then reached for Amanda and strapped her in. Deftly, he folded the stroller and tossed it in the back of the Bronco. Then he jumped into the driver's seat, started the engine, and they roared out of the lot. After they'd driven a few blocks, he handed her something fuzzy and grayish.

''Found this on the floor of the car.''

''Oh, it's Amanda's lamb. It's so dirty, I try to hide it from her—''

From the back seat, Amanda got a glimpse of the lamb and let out a scream.

"Give it to her," Ben suggested.

"But—"

"It's her security, Kate, just what she needs at this point."

Without enthusiasm, Kate handed the stuffed animal to Amanda, who grabbed it with eager hands and immediately put its ear in her mouth.

"Ugh," Kate said. But she admitted relief when the baby made satisfied gooing sounds and then, hugging her lamb, fell asleep, lulled by the rhythm of the car.

They rode in silence, toward what destination Kate didn't know. "Shouldn't we call the police?" she asked finally.

"We will, but I didn't want to hang around. Yours was the only damaged car. Did you notice that?"

She hadn't. She spoke the next words unbelievingly. "Why is someone after me?"

"I can't answer that, Kate," he replied. After a moment he added, "You say you have no enemies. But this isn't the kind of thing a friend would do, is it?" He shot her a dark look.

"No, it isn't. But I don't have any idea what's happening," she insisted, adding adamantly, "This isn't my fault."

"I didn't say it was, Kate."

"I know. I'm just so confused. I appreciate your help. Don't know what I would have done without it. But I have just one more favor," she added, "if you don't mind taking me and Amanda home so I can call the police...."

Ben stopped for a red light. "I'll be glad to, but are you sure you want to go home? Whoever is responsible for all this knows where you work, what car you drive. It's safe to say he probably knows where you live, too."

Kate put her head in her hands. How could this be happening to her?

"Let me take you to a safe place. A friend's house," he suggested.

"I don't know anyone in Denver except Tina and she lives in a one-room efficiency apartment. I doubt if she'd welcome guests, not us, anyway. Maybe a hotel." The idea of being alone in a hotel room wasn't appealing, but it was better than her apartment, especially if what Ben suggested was true.

"Do you think this person wants to kill me?" She couldn't keep the shakiness from her voice.

"Maybe only to frighten you."

"Well, he—or she—is doing one heck of a job. I'm scared to death. Things like this don't happen to people like me," she added defiantly. "And what about Amanda? I'm so worried about her."

Ben reacted to that before he had a chance to think of the consequences. "You're bringing her home with me. Just for the night," he added quickly. "My house is absolutely secure. No one will harm you there. We'll call the police, and tomorrow you can make more permanent plans. How does that sound?"

Ben heard a sigh escape her lips. He couldn't believe he'd made the offer, but it had been necessary. Kate was exhausted and confused, in his estimation in no shape to look after herself or the kid. What kind of man would dump a woman and baby at a hotel when it was obvious that something weird was going on in their lives? That might be the expedient thing to do, but Ben couldn't bring himself to be that heartless.

"Someone's after you, Kate. You can't keep denying that forever."

Kate leaned her head against the soft leather seat. Ben was right. She was in trouble, and his offer sounded wonderful to her, making her feel warm and protected. She wouldn't normally go home with a stranger—well, almost a stranger—but Ben was different. He'd become her protector.

"I don't want to impose," she said miserably. "We should probably go to a hotel—I've caused you enough problems today. Even put you in danger."

"I can take care of myself, Kate. It's you and Amanda I'm worried about. I don't want you to be alone."

She didn't want that either. A long night in a hotel room, wondering if she'd been followed, obsessing about her pursuer, worrying about Amanda. Emotionally, she wanted someone with her; intellectually, she needed a witness to verify what happened to the police. Staying together was the most sensible call in a day that otherwise made no sense.

"Thanks, Ben," she said. "Amanda and I will take you up on your offer. I just hope we won't be a problem."

Ben nodded. One night out of his life. "No problem at all," he said easily.

BEN WOUND ON AND OFF the interstate highways and headed west toward Golden. He checked the rearview mirror to be sure no one was following and then glanced at Kate, who sat silently, staring into the darkness. Amanda was sound asleep. He thought about turning on the radio but decided against it. The peacefulness felt good right now.

"It won't be much longer," he assured her.

Kate nodded. She felt numb. Headlights flashed past in the darkness; the tires of the Bronco hummed on the interstate. They'd passed Golden, and she had no idea where they were going. When he exited onto a side road, she wondered if she'd made the right decision; when he turned onto a snow-packed dirt road, her doubts intensified.

She clutched the armrest as the road curved upward. There was nothing outside but pitch-black night. Even the sky was blocked by the trees that lined their route.

Kate swallowed hard. What the hell had she gotten into? Ben said his house was secure, but this was ridiculous. They'd left civilization for isolation.

Ben shifted gears, and the car lurched forward. "The road gets pretty rough in winter," he said.

"I noticed." She heard her voice, high and nervous.

A dark shape darted across the road. Ben braked, Kate screamed and Amanda woke up with a start. "What—"

"A deer. Guess I didn't tell you I lived in the foothills."

"Foothills?" She felt as if they were at the top of the world—or the end of the world.

"Some people would call them mountains, but technically they're not." He sped up again and rounded a curve. A clearing appeared and a dark shape loomed above them. Kate had only a glimpse of the log house in the headlights before Ben pulled into the garage.

"This is it." He touched a button and the door closed behind them, sealing them off from the night.

Kate opened the car door and got out. She'd really done it now—left Denver's tenuous security to venture into the unknown with a stranger.

What had she been thinking of?

# Chapter Three

"Here we are," he announced as he opened the door and flipped on the light, a modern chandelier that illuminated the huge room. Two stories high, it was built at angles with windows looking out across the moonlit, snow-covered mountains.

"It's—great," she said, looking around. The brightly lit room banished her fears, and curiosity pushed aside her nervousness. Counting the sides of the house, she realized the room was hexagonal. "Fascinating," she added. She stood in the middle of the big room, holding on to Amanda, gaping at the architecture of his home, while Ben took the stairs two at a time.

"I'll be right back," he called out. "Make yourselves at home—you and Mandy."

She watched him disappear onto a balcony at one end of the room.

"There's a closet under the stairs," he called from out of sight.

"Okay," she said, wondering what was happening and where he'd gone. "I'll just hang up our things." She crossed the room on colorful, woven rugs that were scattered over the hardwood floors, and found the closet, cleverly hidden in the redwood structure beneath the staircase. She deposited Amanda on the floor and managed to get out of her soiled coat and hang it up. But the baby wasn't interested in staying put; she was off across the room on all fours, arms and legs pumping furiously.

Kate let her go. She seemed to be heading toward a tall fireplace at the opposite end of the room, but there was a screen in front of it, and the logs were unlit so it didn't pose an immediate threat. Kate followed, glancing occasionally toward the upstairs balcony.

The woven rugs that covered the floors also decorated the walls. They were unique, so much like art objects that Kate felt as if she were in a museum of Native American folklore. Somehow, she was pleased that his heritage was so evident here in this modern hexagonal home.

But where in the world was he?

At that moment, he came down the stairs, carrying blankets and a pillow, which he dropped on a futon near her. "I'll sleep down here. I've put out bedding and nightclothes for you upstairs," he said.

"No," she protested, "it's bad enough to intrude, but we're not going to drive you out of your bed."

Ben stripped off his jacket and tossed it on the futon. "It'll be easier for me to bunk here. I expect to be up late working—"

Kate noticed the banks of computer terminals, monitors and other high-tech equipment that she didn't recognize—all snuggled against one of the walls.

"My office," he said.

"Your house makes quite a statement," she said.

"*And* it's functional. Every one of the six walls has its use," he said, ticking off the angles of the house. "Fireplace, office, kitchen, bath, foyer, and staircase which leads to my bedroom and bath upstairs—yours for the night."

"If you're sure—" she began hesitantly.

His gaze was steady and level. "I wouldn't have suggested the sleeping arrangements if they didn't suit me, Kate."

She nodded mutely. It didn't take more than a few hours with Ben to reinforce the fact that he did what he wanted.

He picked up Amanda and headed for the kitchen. "I'll check out the food supply—"

"I should have thought to ask you to stop at a store," she said. "I have nothing for Amanda."

"That's all right. We'll improvise. Meanwhile, there's a phone in the foyer."

"Phone?"

"To call the police."

"Of course. I'd almost forgotten." The admission was a little embarrassing for her, especially since it could have meant she'd been thinking of other things—the house, even its owner. She hurried toward the foyer.

The call was brief, as she'd expected, and when she returned to the kitchen, he had apparently completed his perusal of the supplies and was tossing Amanda into the air. He turned to her. "A short call, which I imagine means the usual disinterest on the part of the authorities."

"They suggested it was probably a random act of violence and told me to call the automobile club, which I did. They'll meet me there tomorrow. That's how I fared. How about you?''

"Found a package of spaghetti," he said. "I don't suppose Mandy could—"

"If we cut it up, maybe—"

"Great. Let's give it a try." He leaned against the doorjamb, the baby tucked under his arm, looking at Kate with a wry smile. "There's really only room for one person in the kitchen." He stepped aside. "So I won't ask if I can help."

She laughed. "It's a fair trade if you get Amanda out of that snowsuit."

"Done," he said. "The spaghetti's on the counter and there's Parmesan cheese and butter in the refrigerator, salt and pepper and—"

"I'll find everything," she told him.

"And I'll strip the kid down to her overalls and shirt and light a fire to warm this place up."

Kate found herself humming as she worked in the kitchen, a sure sign that she had finally relaxed. And the result of her efforts was actually edible.

"I call it delicious," Ben said, finishing off his spaghetti and dipping a hunk of bread into the residue on his plate. "I'd expected a sprinkling of cheese, but what we have here is—"

"A sort of mock marinara sauce."

"Whatever you call it, here's to the chef," he said, raising his glass.

She clinked her glass against his. "And here's to the wine supplier."

"That was easy. I just opened a bottle, but you created a feast."

Kate laughed. "Thanks for the compliment. Amanda looks pretty satisfied, too."

The baby, propped up in a chair with pillows all around, had devoured her chopped-up spaghetti and a bottle of milk, and was nodding happily, her shirt covered with dinner's residue.

Kate leaned back in her chair in the big living room, warmed by a roaring fire, and looked out on the moonlit panorama. "It's beautiful," she said.

"I wanted a place where I could work and yet feel as if I were outdoors. This room brings the outside in. Wait until you see it in the daylight. The view is spectacular."

Before she got too comfortable, Kate roused herself. "It's time to get the baby bathed and put to bed. I need a shower myself," she added. "It's been quite a day."

"I put out towels."

"Thanks," she said, picking up the drowsing baby.

"I'm assuming that Mandy can sleep in a shirt and diaper."

"Absolutely. And diapers I have plenty of."

"As for your nightclothes—"

"Whoops," she said, "I'd forgotten about myself. Only the clothes on my back."

"I put something out for you that should be—" he looked her up and down before adding "—comfortable."

"Thanks again," she murmured as she scooped up the baby.

Once upstairs, Amanda woke up just long enough for Kate to bathe her, change her diaper and try to get a clean shirt over her head.

"Now, if I could get your arms in those two little holes, you'd be ready for bed," Kate said, struggling, with no help from Amanda, to poke the baby's chubby arms into the arm openings. "I'll never get the hang of this if I live to be a hundred."

"Ma-ma," was the baby's helpful comment. But she finally relaxed enough for Kate to finish the job. In fact, by the time she put the baby in the middle of the bed with pillows all around, Amanda was sound asleep.

"That's what happens after a hard day at the office," Kate said as she headed for the shower.

BEN HAD LAID OUT her nightclothes, a flannel shirt and a pair of white athletic socks. "Hmm. Not too alluring," she said aloud. She couldn't help wondering what he chose for the other women who ended up in his mountain hideaway for the night. Something filmy, probably, from his supply of negligees, the very ones he'd hidden away when he disappeared upstairs earlier.

No, that didn't make sense, she thought, shaking her head. He didn't need a supply of sexy nightwear; the women who came up here with him probably brought along their own—or slept in nothing at all!

"But not me," she said, surveying herself in the mirror. The shirt fit her like a small tent, but it was warm, and so were the socks. She wasn't here to be sexy; she was here to be protected. She checked Amanda one more time before going down the stairs to join Ben.

He was at his computer, his back to her. She moved silently across the room in her sock feet. He seemed intent on his work, and she didn't want to disturb his concentration.

When she got closer, Kate peered over his shoulder. And what she saw froze her in her tracks. Her *life* was there on the screen.

"You're spying on me," she cried.

Ben turned around. "Talk about spying...who's tiptoeing up behind me?"

"That's because I didn't want to bother you. I was being considerate while you—you—"

He waited, an amused look on his face.

"This isn't funny, Ben. Look up there on the screen, it's—"

"The life and times of Katherine Haworth McNair. Take a look for yourself." He moved aside. "Your personnel record from ESS. Education, previous jobs, even stats—height, weight—112?" One dark eyebrow shot up.

"I've gained a little since then," she snapped.

"I don't see any measurements here, though. But I'd guess 34-23-34—"

Kate reddened in anger. "I thought you'd hacker-proofed the ESS files."

"Not for myself. I left a back door open to the headquarters."

She looked at the screen again. "That's not in my ESS file! How in the world did you get my credit card records?"

"One of the tricks of the trade. I've done some work for credit rating firms. You're very responsible," he complimented. "Everything paid and up-to-date. Even your Red Riding Hood coat."

Again, she wasn't amused. "This is an invasion of privacy," she said angrily. "It's bad enough for the credit company to know everything about me, but for a stranger to go in and find out—"

"Stranger? That wounds me, Kate. After all, we've been shot at together, and you're sleeping in my bed, in my shirt—"

"That's not my choice," she cried. Then, hands on hips, she confronted him. "I want to know why you're doing this, why you're prying into my life like some twenty-first-century Peeping Tom. I'm the victim, not the criminal! What's going on here?"

She was angry, really angry, and he found the display of emotion tantalizing. After her bath, she'd let down her hair—both literally and figuratively—and it waved about her face in the most appealing way. She looked softer and more vulnerable in his oversize shirt—in spite of her tough stance. Yet there was also an incandescence about her. Maybe it was the glow of her hair or the backlight of the flames—or the look in her eyes because that was definitely fiery.

He got up and poked at the logs, his movements slow and deliberate, taking his time in answering. He tried to remember if he'd ever had a woman spend the night in his house. Just *spend the night,* nothing more. He couldn't imagine that had ever happened. So this would be a first.

She folded her arms, silently, and he couldn't help thinking how tempting she looked, out of her office, out of that buttoned-up brown suit. He'd promised Kate and the baby a safe place, and he wouldn't go back on that promise. No moves, he cautioned himself.

But as he straightened up, returned the fireplace screen to its place and looked back at her, he couldn't help wondering what she was really like. He doubted if he'd ever know.

"Ben—" She was finally demanding a response.

"All right. I admit that I could have asked you questions about yourself, but it seemed easier to use the computer while you were putting Mandy to sleep. She is asleep, isn't she?"

"In the middle of your bed, with pillows banked all around her. But don't try to distract me with questions about the baby. What's going on?"

Ben chuckled. "Cut to the chase? Okay. But first, how about a brandy to warm you up—or maybe, in your case, to cool you down."

Kate agreed, settling on his sofa and tucking her legs beneath her. Her face was still wary, and the anger hadn't left her green eyes. Ben handed her a brandy, and she took a long swallow.

"All right. I'm cool. Now explain, please."

"It's simple. I wanted to know more about you."

She looked at him over the rim of her brandy snifter. "How come I'm not flattered by the sound of that?"

"I don't mean to flatter you. I mean to find out about you so I can understand what's happening."

"You could have asked," she said.

"You might not have told me everything."

"Wait a minute. Why *should* I tell you everything? I hardly know you."

"Exactly. We've known each other for only a few hours. And in that time you've been shot at and your tires have been slashed. A week earlier, someone pushed you in front of a car—"

"Accident," she cut in. And then she added more thoughtfully, "Maybe."

Ben sat in a low chair across from her. "I'm thinking the same thing you are. Too many accidents. Too many coincidences, no matter what our overburdened police force may say."

Kate took another sip of brandy and then put the glass down. "I haven't tried to put it all together, connect everything. I didn't want to because the scenario seems so...sinister."

"It could be," he told her.

"I know," she admitted. "But I don't know why. All I can do is repeat what I told the police. I don't have any enemies—"

"That you know of." He leaned toward her, a serious expression on his face. "Don't you understand, Kate? That's why I was delving into your past—to find out if there was something you'd missed—or forgotten about or thought wasn't important."

"Or lied about?" She looked at him with a level gaze.

"We all like to present ourselves in the best way possible, Kate."

"There's nothing," she said flatly.

"There must be," he insisted. "No one goes through life without making waves of some kind."

"I'm afraid I did," she said a little apologetically. "My background is unremarkable. I'm an only child. My parents are in Kenya—"

At his questioning look, she explained. "My father is a career diplomat." She watched for his reaction to that. "Thirty years in the foreign service. No government intrigue, Ben."

"I didn't say anything."

"You didn't have to. When the foreign service is mentioned, people always think about mysterious goings-on, but believe me, my parents are very dedicated and loyal. Even a little boring."

"When did you last see them?" he asked.

"Two years ago when they were on home leave. I didn't visit them in Kenya."

Ben sighed. "That brings us back to you." He downed his brandy. "Boyfriends—present or ex?"

"None who wish me harm. I have no idea where most of the guys I dated are now, but I was only serious with one man in my life. We broke up before I moved to Phoenix. He's since married and has a baby. So I seriously doubt if he'd want to kill me." She let out a sigh. "*Kill* me. God, that sounds so sinister."

"But we have to consider it, Kate."

"I suppose so." She felt like asking for another brandy but decided against it. A clear head was what she needed as they reviewed her life.

He pressed on. "Former jobs?"

"I beat out a couple of people at ESS for my promotion to Phoenix. A couple more for my move here. But getting rid of me wouldn't have meant that any of them would get the job. They all had other career possibilities within—and without—the company. Everyone I know is too damn career-minded to take the time to wipe me out." She gave a small shaky laugh. "I sound like a character in a bad detective novel, don't I?"

He smiled. From what he'd seen of her, he had no trouble believing the career-minded bit. Above all, she had success uppermost in her mind.

"Then let's look at Denver," Ben said, returning to his keyboard. "We'll start with the most recent clients." He tapped a series of keys, and waited a few seconds. Then he printed out a copy of the list on the screen and handed it to Kate. "Anything suspicious going on with any of these companies?"

She took the list from him. "So you left a back door into my ESS office, too," she commented sarcastically as she glanced at the client names.

"I'll close it up when we figure out what's going on."

"If anything *is* going on."

"Kate, think carefully. Do any of them have it in for you?"

She studied the list of the most recent ESS clients. "I've placed executives with the first three. National Trust of Denver, Arrington Oil and Benjamin Investment. They're cream-of-the-crop companies. They don't shoot at a person for being a successful headhunter."

"Headhunter?" He leaned back in his chair, hands behind his neck. The gestures tightened the muscle across his chest and made his shoulders appear even broader. The firelight flickered a golden glaze across his forehead and cheek, and for a moment she almost lost her cool. Quickly, she caught herself.

"Headhunter is a slang term for companies like ESS that find people to fill top-management jobs."

"So you're a headhunter?" He chuckled, turning back to the computer. "And they're all satisfied with your placements?"

"As far as I know."

"Did anyone lose out on a job? Some applicant you sent out who got turned down by one of those companies?"

"Sure, but wouldn't they take it out on the company who didn't hire them instead of on me? After all, I'm the good guy."

"No nutcases?"

"No obvious ones. Just men and women who want to work. They're usually registered at other placement agencies, too. Honestly, I haven't ruined anyone's life recently."

"Okay, scratch your applicants and the companies you've placed with. Let's look carefully at the other companies on the list, the ones you're still 'headhunting' for." He tried to hide his smile. "Start with appointments you made a week before the first accident when you were pushed in front of the car."

"I can't remember anything unusual at all. I called for appointments. I made visits. The dates are here on the lists." She consulted her hard copy while he watched the screen. "I did have a couple of appointments," she said, remembering, "that were kind of odd."

"Odd?" He looked back at her.

"They were both at night. One put me off when I got there and the other one didn't show."

"Now we're getting somewhere," said. "Tell me about them."

Relieved that he was back at the screen and she didn't have to look at his fabulous abs, she told him, "One was the woman I mentioned to you, Coral Lampiere. She was a teacher at the private school I attended. We kept in touch and when I moved here we had lunch. She wanted ESS to help replace some staff at Sky-High Spa...."

"Nothing unusual about that."

"Nope," she agreed. "Then we made an appointment for nine-thirty at night."

"Now *that's* unusual."

Kate shook her head. "You've admitted not knowing much about workout clubs, and you don't," she

added with a laugh. "These places open early and
don't close until nine o'clock. That's the logical time
for Coral to set her appointments. During the day,
there's just too much going on."

She was thoughtful for a long moment, remembering. "What *was* unusual was that Coral never
showed," she told him. "The whole building was deserted except for the janitor, who was no help at all. I
waited for a while and then finally left. When I called
the next day to follow up, I was told Coral had gone
on vacation."

"Annoying," Ben commented, "but hardly sinister. You saw nothing?"

"Only what I told you. No drug deals, no shady
characters lurking in the shadows at Sky-High Spa."
Kate was becoming irritated. "This is getting us nowhere."

Ben held up a conciliatory hand. "Tell me about
your other evening appointment."

Kate checked her list. Robert Brownley of United
Charities. "It wasn't really an appointment. I was
supposed to drop off a contract, but he wasn't in the
office. Because I wanted to get started on the search
for his executive assistant the next morning, I took the
contract by his house. It was dinnertime, and I think
he and his wife were having cocktails. He was in a
hurry, and so was I. Nothing sinister."

"Did he seem irritated?"

"Maybe a little gruff, but it was after office hours,
so I figured he just wanted to get back to his private
life. Can't blame him."

Ben shrugged. "Your clients don't seem to be
minding their stores very well, but other than that, I
don't see anything sinister either. I'll run computer

checks on both of them. Didn't you call this Coral woman something else?''

"When she taught my dance class in private school, she was Carol Lampson. She changed her name when she opened the spa.'' Kate shrugged off his interested look. "Lots of people know that, so I don't think she shot at me to keep her name change a secret.''

Ben was thoughtful for a moment. "Maybe we're looking at this from the wrong angle.'' He changed programs on his computer. "When did you come to Denver?''

"Six weeks ago—the first part of November.''

"When did you get custody of Mandy?''

"Temporary guardianship,'' she corrected. "Last week. I had just come back to work from the the the accident—''

He lifted an eyebrow.

"Or whatever you want to call it,'' she corrected, "and that afternoon a lawyer called to tell me Amanda was on the way.''

"That was the first you heard?''

"Oh, no. Her parents died in the airplane crash before Thanksgiving, but the baby stayed with a family friend until the will was read and the lawyers made arrangements to send her here. Poor Amanda,'' she said. "Losing her parents and not knowing why, and then being shuttled from place to place. It's a miracle she's coped as well as she has.''

Ben was concentrating on the computer, and Kate wondered if he'd been listening to her. "Why did you want to know all those details?'' she asked.

"Look.'' He moved aside so she could see the screen where he had created a triangular design. He placed the cursor on one corner and typed "December 15.''

"Today's date. You were shot at, and someone slashed your tires. Now, let's go back, what, ten days, to December 5?"

She nodded.

He typed that date at another corner. "You were hit by the car—either on purpose or accidentally—on about that date. Then Mandy arrived. How many days later?"

"Three," she answered.

He typed "December 8" at the apex of the triangle. And in the middle he typed "Amanda." "Do you see what's happened?"

"You think all this has to do with *Amanda?*" she asked unbelievingly.

"Think about it." He got up slowly and stretched. "You say nothing unusual happened at work. Your clients are above reproach. You've got no skeletons in your closet. But *something* has changed in your life recently, and that's Mandy." He pointed to the diagram on the computer screen. "In the center is Mandy."

She sat down, confused. "Why would someone want me out of the way because of the baby?"

"Aha, Dr. Watson, *that's* the question," he answered. "If we find the answer, we'll discover who the hell is after you."

"I can't believe—" she began tentatively.

"It's logical, Kate." He prodded. "Who, besides you, knew about Mandy?"

"Plenty of people," she answered. "All of Libby's friends back east, the couple who kept the baby after the plane crash, some cousins in Florida." She closed her eyes, trying to think.

"What about here in Denver?" he asked.

"No one," she said, "except the lawyer, Daniel Hedrick."

"A good place to start," Ben said, refocusing his attention on the computer. "I'll log into a law library through the Internet and get American Bar Association records. I can find out what kind of cases he handles and then look into his personal life, including his credit records."

"Just like you did with me..."

"Exactly," he replied, intent on the screen. "More brandy?" he asked over his shoulder.

"No, I'm fine." She felt warm and relaxed, in spite of all the confusion, the puzzles that Ben had created on screen—and in her head. Her edgy nerves and racing mind were gradually slowing, thanks to the combination of her bath, the fire and the brandy.

She glanced around the room, seeing again the wall hangings that had intrigued her and suddenly changing the subject. "Those hangings—are they Cheyenne?"

"A few of them," he replied. "But there're also Arapaho and Nez Percé as well as some eastern tribes—Cherokee, Creek and Seminole. Collecting them is my hobby." He turned and gave her a mocking look. "I like to keep in touch with my Native American roots."

Without waiting for her response to that, he was back at work, his fingers skimming the keyboard. Kate watched in fascination. What an interesting dichotomy he was. His technology was out of the twenty-first century, but he hadn't forsaken his past. Ben's heritage seemed a natural part of him, and yet he neither overdramatized nor downplayed it.

Now he was hunting down whoever had shot at them, not in an exotic Native American setting but on the computer.

Was he on the right track, she wondered, about the attacks on her life? *Did* they have something to do with Amanda? She couldn't believe that was possible, but as Ben pointed out, it was logical. Before Amanda, her life had been centered around her work. After Amanda, everything had changed.

She closed her eyes and realized suddenly that she was too tired to open them again. She'd had every intention of getting up and going to bed. But it felt too good to lie on the sofa and bask in the warmth of the fire. She had meant to help Ben by concentrating on his triangle and the dates when the incidents occurred.

She tried to remember. December 5. What else had happened on that day? Something... She couldn't focus on it.

And then today, December 15, her appointment with Ben... the gunshots... the tires slashed...

Waves of exhaustion washed over Kate, drawing her deeper into its depths. Unable to concentrate, she slipped slowly toward sleep, into a soft enveloping blackness. Then it came to her, and she remembered what else had happened on December 5.

AFTER HALF AN HOUR of intense concentration, Ben turned away from the computer and started to speak. Seeing Kate, he bit back his words.

She was sound asleep, lying on her side with one hand under her cheek, red hair tousled around her face. Her breathing was deep and regular, the sleep of exhaustion. His flannel shirt, which swallowed her in a very appealing way, had slid halfway up her thigh and exposed an expanse of smooth white skin.

Ben felt a familiar tightening in his loins. Hell, just because she was good-looking and lying on his sofa and wearing nothing but a flannel shirt, was no reason for him to give in, no reason for him to relinquish his original decision to stay cool in the heat of the excitement she generated.

But he had to move her, and he didn't want to bother her. That could be a problem. No, he decided, it would be safer to wake her up.

He leaned over and lightly touched her hair. "Kate..."

She made a little moaning sound and snuggled more deeply into the sofa. But she didn't wake up.

"Okay," he said softly, "you win—and I tuck you in." He lifted her, and she stirred, mumbling something unintelligible, but her eyes remained closed.

Trying to steel himself against her obvious charms, he settled her warmly into his arms. He could feel the curve of her breast against his chest and her soft breath against his cheek. Those were the very stimulations he could do without. Taking a deep breath of his own he headed for the stairs, climbed them quickly and went into his room. There was a low light on beside the bed where Amanda was sleeping, her thumb tucked tightly into her mouth.

Carefully, Ben placed Kate on the bed, rearranged Amanda and her wall of pillows, and covered both of them with a quilt. Kate moaned again, opened her eyes to about half-mast and looked at him without recognition. "What—"

"It's okay," he replied. "Go back to sleep."

She immediately closed her eyes and was breathing deeply in a few seconds. Better, safer, he thought as he reached for the light, ready to turn it off. But something stopped him, the compelling picture of the two of them sleeping, so lovely, so innocent, so...

"No way," he murmured. "Just because it's holiday time, and she's alone with a baby, doesn't mean I'm getting sentimental. Save that for the Christmas cards," he told himself.

He turned off the light and went downstairs to sleep—or try to.

# Chapter Four

Kate woke with a start. Where was she? In a strange room, a strange bed! Then she remembered. She and Amanda were sharing the upstairs room in Ben's house. Another bizarre situation in more than a week of weird happenings.

But at least the baby had slept. And slept. She couldn't believe how long. "Amanda," she said softly, turning over and searching among the pillows.

She sat up with a start. The baby was gone!

Kate's feet hit the floor with a thud. Where could she be? Under the bed? In the bathroom? The door was closed so she couldn't have gotten out and fallen down the stairs. Unless... Could someone have stolen the baby during the night?

She rushed to the bedroom door and threw it open, shouting, "Amanda, Amanda—" Whoever had shot at her and Ben, slashed the tires, could have taken the baby. Or maybe— She thought of the revelation that had come to her just before sleep. "No," she told herself. "No!"

She had just started down the stairs when Ben responded from below. "Amanda's down here, Kate—with me."

"Oh, thank God." She flew down the stairs.

Ben stood in front of the fireplace, holding the baby, who was happily sucking on a bottle.

With a sigh, Kate sank onto the sofa. It took her a minute to recover. "I thought...someone had...taken her."

"No way, Kate. Not in my house," Ben assured. "Everyone's safe here."

"I couldn't imagine anything else. I'd thought about locking the door, even barricading the stairway in case she got out of the room somehow. But I don't remember doing it. I—oh," she said as it hit her.

He raised one dark eyebrow.

"I fell asleep on the sofa."

"You sure did."

Automatically, Kate's hand went to the neck of the shirt. His shirt. The top button had come undone during the night. "How embarrassing," she said.

He didn't respond, but there it was again. Damn that eyebrow. Up it went.

"I mean...to be put to bed like a child," she added quickly.

"It was my pleasure," Ben replied. "I actually tried to wake you, but you were dead to the world."

"Thanks," Kate said, relaxing. Or trying to. That one nagging thought kept at her. "I need to ask you about—something."

"Sure. But first—how about coffee?"

She nodded. "I should probably change the baby."

"Been done," he told her proudly.

"Thanks," she repeated. "You're better with Amanda than I." She couldn't believe how easily Ben handled the child, how content—and calm—Amanda seemed in his arms.

"Experience," he replied. "And maybe she senses I'm at ease. There's cereal," he said as he poured the coffee and handed it to her.

Their fingers touched over the cup in a gesture that made the morning seem intimate. A man and a woman sharing breakfast. A baby in his arms. The woman still in her nightclothes. Too intimate, she thought, for someone she knew nothing about.

Ben leaned back in his chair and looked across at her. "Okay, what gives? There's something on your mind."

*He* was on her mind, but what she was thinking kept getting mixed up with what she was seeing, his physical presence. It dominated everything. He was wearing boots, well-washed jeans and a plaid shirt. He hadn't shaved, but he was the kind of man who looked good with a day's growth of beard. She wished she had a robe—a blanket—*something* to give her protection from Ben's nearness. She was very aware of him and his eyes on her, measuring as if he knew she was uncomfortable around him. And why.

She simply couldn't talk to him dressed like this. Standing up, she said, "Yes, something is on my mind, but let me change before we talk. I'd feel more—comfortable." Without waiting for a reply, she took her coffee and went upstairs.

*Now* SHE WAS in charge, Kate decided when she returned, dressed in her brown suit, her hair in a reasonable facsimile of a French twist. Ben was still at the table, on his second cup of coffee. Amanda had finished her breakfast and was on the floor, blissfully tearing the pages from an old catalog.

Kate put down her empty cup, and he refilled it.

"I'm waiting," he said slowly.

She took a sip of coffee and sat opposite him. "It's about you."

He cocked that dark eyebrow again.

"Last night you asked me **to** try and think of anything unusual that might connect the incidents...the attacks. And I did think of something." He watched her silently, but she didn't lose her cool this time. "On both days—when I was pushed in front of the car and when I was shot at—I had appointments. With you."

"So," he said. "You think I could be involved in a sinister plot?"

"You *asked* me to think of everything," she shot back.

"All right, let's explore this. Where was I when you were shot at?"

"With me," she said softly.

"And when you were hit by the car?"

"In my office, I suppose, waiting—"

"With Tina," he added. "'Course, I could have masterminded the whole thing and had someone else carry out the dirty deeds."

"I'm not saying you did anything, but I wondered last night. I still do."

"Sometimes coincidence is just that, Kate. I have no reason to harm you, but if I wanted to, haven't I had ample opportunity, alone in my house with you all night?"

She nodded.

"Two things, Kate. Number one, you're right to be suspicious. From now on, I want you to suspect everyone. Number two," he added with a grin, "don't *tell* the person you suspect!"

She felt her face redden.

"Come on, loosen up. I'm teasing, but you could have gotten into a lot of trouble if you'd been right about me."

"I guess I never did believe it, or I wouldn't have told you. That *was* stupid of me, though."

"You're not a detective, Kate. You're a headhunter," he added with another grin. "So be careful." He picked up a sheaf of printouts from the computer. "I'm not a detective, either, but I'm pretty good at snooping. And I can't resist a puzzle. I did some research on Daniel Hedrick last night. He handles family law—divorces, custody hearings, that sort of thing. Low-profile type of guy. Except..."

"Except?"

"He's in trouble financially. Recently married a woman with very expensive tastes. Plus, two ex-wives and three kids to support. The bottom line is, he needs money."

"How would getting rid of me help his finances?"

"Let's tinker with the idea," Ben said thoughtfully. "If something happened to you, what would become of Amanda?"

"I suppose she'd go to my second cousin in Florida. I hardly know her and her husband, but other than my parents, they're the closest relatives." She caught on to his scenario. "Are you thinking that Hedrick might want to get Amanda to..." She paused. "To... what?"

"I have no idea. That's why I'd like to meet this guy, check him out myself." He laughed sardonically. "I know this is none of my business, but—"

"You were also shot at—*and* got stuck with me and Amanda. Besides, you can't resist a puzzle."

"Exactly. I like to know how things work and why. And this is one hell of a mystery."

Kate got down on the floor beside Amanda, who was stuffing bits of brightly colored catalog pages into her mouth. "I don't find it all that fascinating, because it's totally messing up my life." As she removed the pages from the baby's hands and mouth, Amanda began to fret. "I wonder if the police will call back about my car."

"Don't count on any suspects being rounded up."

Amanda was into major fussing and on the verge of tears.

"Maybe she'd like her lamb," Ben suggested. "I threw it in the wash this morning. Should be dry by now."

"Thank you," Kate said guiltily. Once again, Ben was proving to be the better parent.

When she returned, Amanda was in Ben's arms at the window where he was showing her the birds gathered at a feeder in the yard. He was right about the morning view. It was breathtaking. The snow-filled trees seemed weighted down with their white burden, ghostly figures shimmering in the morning sun. In the distance, the jagged peaks of the Continental Divide stood like cutouts against the blue sky.

Kate waited awhile before reaching for the telephone and breaking into the quiet moment. "I guess I'd better call Tina and tell her I'll be late."

Ben turned from the window. "I don't think you should go to the office, Kate. How do you know the shooter won't come back?"

She put down the phone. "I don't," she said slowly. "This—person—could come to the office—or to my apartment." She clenched her fists in anger. "Do you realize what's happening? My life is being stolen by some nameless, faceless maniac.''

She began pacing in front of Amanda and Ben. "I'm not going to let it happen. No one is going to treat me like this and get away with it.'' She stopped and shook her fist. "Do you hear me?''

Amanda's eyes widened and her mouth formed a perfect little O.

"We hear you, loud and clear, General. We're waiting for your next move,'' Ben replied.

"All right. Here it is. I'll go to Denver. Get a temporary place to live. Hire a baby-sitter, and conduct business by fax and phone until the police do something. I'm calling Tina to tell her. Business as usual. Except I won't be in the office.'' She shrugged. "A minor inconvenience that we can deal with.''

She picked up the phone again and punched in numbers as she talked. "Then, I'll make a couple of ESS calls before we go to town—that is, if you'll take us—''

"I don't expect you and Amanda to walk back to Denver.''

When Kate reached Tina and told her where she was, her secretary responded to the news with a low laugh and an envious remark. "Way to go, boss.'' Kate ignored that, gave instructions, picked up messages and moved on to the next call, quickly, efficiently, arranging to meet the tow truck driver and hand over her keys.

As Ben watched with a mixture of admiration and amusement, Kate pulled out her day planner and began making notes. "Rent an apartment, hire a sitter, pick up some baby food, buy enough clothes to get me through the next few days—and oh, yes,'' she added casually, "find out who tried to run me down, shot at me and slashed my tires. Just an average day in the life of a single, working mom."

"You're handling this well, Kate," he complimented.

"What choice do I have?"

Their eyes met, and he saw once more the vulnerability there. Deep down, she was scared—as well she should be—but he had to admire her courage.

"Now on to business. Coral Lampiere at Sky-High Spa...then Robert Brownley of United Charities." As she made the calls, Ben saw Kate slip into her young executive mode, which she wore very easily, a tiger at work. Last night she was a vulnerable, sexy woman; today she was all business. As for her mothering ability—Ben looked at Amanda, happily chewing on the lamb's ear—she had a long way to go.

Coral was still on vacation; Brownley wasn't in, either, but Kate plunged ahead, calling his home. After a brief conversation, she hung up with a grin. "Brownley's at a breakfast meeting, but he *signed* the contract! His wife has it, ready for me to pick up."

"Headhunter on the loose," Ben quipped.

"Without a car. Maybe I should rent one."

"Where do they live?" he asked.

She looked at her notes. "Country Club section, Third and High."

"Closer than the car rental. And I'd feel better in the driver's seat, keeping an eye on you."

"Thanks, Ben. If you'll stuff Amanda into her snowsuit, I'll get my coat—"

"Leave it, Kate. The coat's like a beacon. Besides, it's dirty, remember?" Ben rummaged through the closet and pulled out a woman's leather jacket. "This should fit you."

"You sure it's all right?" She couldn't control her inner curiosity. Whose coat was it? An ex-girlfriend—or maybe not even *ex?*

"Let's say the owner was passing through town. She won't be back for it."

He helped Kate into the coat, and stayed close, his hand on her shoulder. She immediately forgot about the coat's owner as she tried to control her heartbeat. Useless, when he was standing so near. Then he touched her hair, and Kate caught her breath. She had to get out of this house and away from the intimacy—and soon!

"This hair...so damned red."

"Sorry," she breathed.

"Don't be. It's fabulous. But it's just like your coat, lighting the way for the person after you. I'll get you a cap to cover it. This person, whoever he—or she—is, could be anywhere."

"I know," she said softly. Despite the brave words and organizational skills she'd demonstrated, she felt fear oppressing her again. At that moment, she wanted nothing more than to stay in the safety of his house.

No, she *did* want more—the comfort of his arms.

He tucked a lock of her hair behind her ear, gave her a well-worn baseball cap and stepped away. "I'll get the kid into her snowsuit."

"Someone in the family had money," Ben said as they pulled into the driveway of Brownley's house. It was similar to other massive brick homes in Country Club, set on rolling lawns with towering trees but even more palatial. "And this guy works for a nonprofit group. Are you sure he's legit?"

Kate shrugged. "Hey, I'm new in town. Maybe you should check him out on your computer. Meanwhile, I want that contract." She opened the car door.

Ben reached out and pulled off the baseball cap. "In this neighborhood, you'll make a better first impression without the Denver Rockies."

The massive front door was opened by a petite woman in her late fifties wearing an expensive running suit, a stylish haircut and a friendly smile. "Kate McNair?"

"Yes. I'm here to see Mrs. Brownley—" Kate glanced over the woman's shoulder into the living room.

"I'm Martha Brownley."

"Yes, of course." Kate tried not to show her surprise. "Mr. Brownley left a contract for me—"

"Come in, my dear, out of the cold."

Ben watched the friendly scene from the car, saw the door close behind the two women and figured they'd be awhile. With a shrug, he gave in to Amanda's cries for entertainment.

When Kate emerged, the older woman was beside her. It amazed Ben how easily women made friends. Together they approached the car, chatting amicably.

Ben opened the door on the passenger side, and Mrs. Brownley peered in. "Oh, what a darling child." After fifteen minutes of Ben's undivided attention, Amanda was laughing happily. "Girl or boy?"

"Girl," Ben replied as Amanda looked up innocently at Kate and said, "Ma-ma, ma-ma," again and again.

"You have a lovely family, Mr. McNair."

"Blackeagle," Kate corrected quickly. "Ben Blackeagle, this is Martha Brownley."

"So pleased to meet you, Mr. Blackeagle. I'll never catch on to modern marriages, women keeping their names, men..." She stopped short of commenting on Ben's ponytail and earring.

"It's not really a modern—" Kate attempted before Ben broke in.

"I'm encouraging Kate to be her own person."

Kate decided not to bother with attempting further explanation. "We'd better be going. We've taken up enough of your time, Mrs. Brownley."

"Nonsense. Besides, I have a marvelous idea," Mrs. Brownley responded. "Why don't the three of you come by Cherry Creek Mall for our Christmas Fest?"

"No, we couldn't possibly—"

"Oh, do, please. It's United Charities' biggest fundraiser. Many of the UC staff will be there. It's a marvelous opportunity for you to meet them, get to know the kind of people Rob hires in his organization."

And get to know Rob himself, Kate thought, deciding then and there to go. "If Ben has the time. My car's in the shop, and he's spending his whole day driving me around."

Ben's expression was unreadable, but his voice was edged with irony. "Sure, I'd like to have some more quality time with my family. It's as if we hardly know each other these days."

"Fabulous. You know where the mall is. We'll be in the fountain area outside Foley's. Santa will be there with his helpers. There's a train for the children, and a trip to Santa's workshop. Your baby will love it."

"We look forward to it," Kate said.

"The fun begins early!" Martha responded cheerfully.

Ben started the engine, and Kate waved goodbye as they drove off.

"Women," he said, shaking his head. "Bonding instantly. Now what was that all about?"

Kate waited until they turned onto Third Street before replying. "She's not his wife!"

"You mean that nice woman is an impostor? What's she doing in Brownley's house?"

"No, *she's* the real Mrs. B., a petite blonde in her late fifties. The woman I saw when I delivered the contracts that night wasn't his wife. She was a tall brunette about thirty years younger. Robert Brownley is having an affair, and I caught him!"

"Maybe the woman you saw was his daughter."

"Nope. The only daughter lives in Spokane. Mrs. Brownley just returned from a two-week visit to see her grandchildren. She told me all about that trip."

"His secretary?"

"Sure. Taking dictation in a negligee over cocktails? Give me a break." Kate narrowed her eyes and chewed on her lower lip. "You know what this means, don't you?"

"That Brownley has a mistress."

"*And* that I saw them together. He could be the one who tried to shoot us."

"Hold on, Kate, let's get logical here."

"Okay," Kate said. "First, Martha has all the money."

"How do you figure that?"

"Their house—it was her family home."

"She told you," Ben said with a grin.

"And I didn't even ask," she replied.

"You're getting to be quite a detective." Stopping at an intersection, he put the baseball cap back on and tucked the escaping hair under the brim. "For safety, just in case your Brownley theory is wrong."

But Kate wouldn't be distracted. "I figure she had an enormous inheritance that Brownley has shared all these years. Enter the sexy mistress. A dangerous situation. If Martha got wind of it, she'd kick him out, ruin his reputation and leave him with only his United Charities' salary, which, you've already noted, is probably minimal."

"It makes sense on a simplistic level. But let's get more sophisticated. Is Brownley the type to stalk you?"

"Can't answer because I've hardly met the man, which is why I want to go to the mall. Confront him—"

"A dangerous idea."

"Think about it, Ben. He's not going to try anything with his wife there."

"Maybe not. But he's also not going to break down and confess the way they do on TV, Kate."

"But at least I'll be acting instead of passively waiting to be attacked again. Maybe I'll get a clue from him—body language or something." At Ben's skeptical look, she snapped, "Any other bright ideas?"

"Except for Hedrick, not a one. We need to shop for you, pick up a few things for Amanda, and the mall's as good a place as any, so why not? Our little warm and loving family at the Christmas Fest."

"Sorry about that family thing, but Martha assumed we were married. And now that you mention it, weren't you the one who—"

"Guilty. And willing to play along for a while. Who knows, it might be fun."

BUT HE DIDN'T HAVE to do it. Ben knew that. After they waited for more than an hour for a delayed tow truck, he could have dropped Kate and Amanda at a car rental place and let them go to the mall on their own, find an apartment and get on with their lives. Instead, he was on his way to see Santa Claus—and liking it. His adrenaline was pumping, and he felt a sense of excitement about the past twenty-four hours.

His enthusiasm lessened when they entered the noisy and crowded mall. Hundreds of children ran madly up and down the escalators, along the promenades and through the stores with harried parents trailing behind, trying to round them up before they zeroed in on the Santa Claus booth.

"There's Mrs. B.," Kate announced when they spotted the UC booth. "I wonder where he is?"

A smiling Martha Brownley waved them over. "I'm so glad you made it. There're lots of UC people at the booth."

"Your husband?" Kate looked around.

Martha shook her head. "Couldn't make it. He's been so busy recently...." Her voice trailed off. "But I'll be glad to introduce you to the others, Kate."

"No, thanks, I'll be fine on my own." Dutifully, Kate headed for the booth, leaving Ben and Amanda in Mrs. B.'s care.

"I do so admire career women," Martha told Ben as they watched Kate walk away. "Especially working mothers. Kate's lucky to have a husband who helps out. You're wonderful with the baby."

As if on cue, Amanda chimed in with a stream of da-das.

"She's quite a handful," Ben replied. "I'm finding myself doing all sorts of things I never imagined." He smiled ruefully.

"I just bet you are," Martha agreed, as Amanda, fascinated by the mall Christmas tree, greedily reached for its decorations, straining in Ben's arms. "Her first Christmas?"

He had no idea. Had Amanda turned one yet or was her birthday just ahead? He decided to tell Martha what she wanted to hear. "Her very first."

"Then we must get your picture with Santa Claus." She looked around and spied Kate at the booth. "Come over here, dear, as soon as you're finished." To Ben she confided, "I'm going to pull rank and put you at the front of the line. Won't a Christmas picture be a wonderful memento?"

Ben decided his only choice was to comply, and by the time Kate joined them, Martha was busy setting up the photo.

"Sorry," Kate mouthed as she slipped in line beside Ben. "These situations keep getting out of hand—"

"No problem. Did you make any good contacts?"

"Not really. Just low-level staff, handing out brochures. How's Amanda's dad?"

"Fine, if only he knew his kid's birthday! Had to fake it."

"She'll be a year old January second—two weeks."

Ben beamed. "Guessed right."

Martha bustled over. "You're next," she told them. "First Amanda on Santa's knee—"

Kate gave the baby's hair a quick comb and then waited for her to shriek with fear as they approached Santa. His heavy and very obviously fake beard was pretty scary stuff, but Amanda seemed to love it. She went eagerly to him, her eyes big and round, and tugged with vigor on the beard.

"I can't believe it's staying on," Kate said, laughing, as the photographer snapped away.

"Adorable," Martha joined in. "Now the whole family."

"I don't think so," Kate responded quickly. "Ben's in a hurry, and—"

"I have plenty of time, sweetheart," Ben said wickedly. "Especially for a holiday picture of our family."

Before she could reply, they were posed alongside Santa. After a couple of shots, the photographer advised, "You folks are supposed to be a happy family enjoying Christmas. Let's make it a little more lively."

Kate forced a smile and turned toward the baby, who giggled on cue. Ben smiled back. Then with a wink, he leaned forward and kissed Kate enthusiastically on the mouth.

# Chapter Five

Kate's eyes opened wide and then snapped shut. This was some kiss. No little peck, no fake for the camera; it was simply delicious! *Anyone* would respond to such a kiss, and Kate certainly did.

Ben's mouth was possessive and insistent, and when hers opened instinctively, she felt his tongue graze her lips. Warmth radiated along her skin, and her heart fluttered wildly before she remembered where they were—and why.

She was on a mission to find Brownley. Martha, Santa, all the rest were incidental. So was the kiss. She pulled away from Ben, trying to pretend that she was unaffected, but she could feel the color flaming in her cheeks.

"Shall we try that again?" Ben called out to the photographer. He'd meant the kiss to be lighthearted, a joke in keeping with the charade performed for Mrs. B. It had turned into something deeper. Sweet and intriguing, there'd been an underlying hint of passion. And he wasn't joking when he asked to try it again.

Before the photographer could answer, Kate responded. "No! I mean, I'm sure it was fine." Under her breath, she whispered to Ben, "Why did you do that?"

"Because I wanted to," he answered. "And because I liked it. I think Mrs. B. did, too." He smiled disarmingly as she approached.

"It's wonderful to see a couple so in love," she said.

"Does it show?" Ben asked with such boyish charm that Kate almost choked.

"It most certainly does," Martha replied. "I'm sure you'll cherish the picture for years to come. We'll mail it to you if you'll just give me your address—and a check, of course. All the profits go to charity," she added.

Kate looked at Ben and batted her eyes coquettishly. "This can be *your* treat, darling," she said, "since you came up with such an original pose."

He kept a straight face. "My pleasure, honey. Maybe you'd like more than one copy. It's for a good cause, you know."

"No, one will be more than enough," she said, fluttering her lashes again. "But I'm sure Martha would appreciate it if you'd add a large donation for United Charities."

Damn. She was good, he thought. "Of course, sweetheart."

This could go back and forth all day, Kate realized, deciding—as Ben busied himself with the unexpected check-writing—to get on to the business at hand. "When do you expect your husband to get here, Martha?"

"He may not make it at all, but I'm still hoping," she replied. "Another board meeting. Rob has so many involvements."

Kate managed a tight smile. He certainly did! "He's lucky to have you to pinch-hit," she said fervently as Amanda squirmed in her arms. "I'll stop by later in case he shows up, but right now, I think it's past time for lunch."

"I recommend Mile-High Grill," Martha suggested. "The mall's a crowded madhouse today, but it's always quiet there, and the food is good."

"Thanks," said Kate, who had very little experience with Denver restaurants—especially the mall variety. A quiet restaurant with good *adult* food sounded like heaven to her.

"What do you think?" she asked Ben.

"I say go with Mrs. B.'s choice."

"Great," she said, "*if* you take the baby."

Ben held out his arms, and Amanda went to him, but not as enthusiastically as usual. She was in a crying mode.

"Fits right in with the general mood," he said, looking around. The mall was crowded with families, parents and kids, none very happy, if their cries were any indication. More candy was thrown on the floor than eaten, more soft drinks spilled than drunk.

"The joys of parenthood," he said. "Demonstrated everywhere."

"Once we get into our restaurant, it'll be different. No kids. No noise. No spills."

"But will they let us in with Amanda?" he wondered.

"'Course."

"Then what makes you think other people with children won't be there, too?"

"Because *they* think they should take their kids to the fast-food places. *We* think we should take our kid—I mean, my kid—I mean—" She stumbled.

"You mean, Amanda."

"Yes—to the best restaurant. And here it is." They pushed through the door and found themselves in a cozy spot, intimate and quiet, very much adults-only. Then Amanda let out a shriek and everyone turned to look at them—as they backed out the door, plans squelched.

"I saw a fast-food place back there..." Ben offered.

"Not Jerry's In and Out, fast-food burgers and dogs?"

"Has a real Amanda ring to it."

He was right, Kate decided when they arrived at Jerry's and found a table. Next to them a toddler burst into tears after spilling his soft drink. The sticky liquid ran across the table and puddled on the floor. His mother hardly noticed; she was too busy wiping mustard off an older child's jacket.

"More joys of parenthood," Ben commented softly. "Now, what'll it be?"

"Whatever's fastest and most filling," she replied, taking the squirming baby from him. Amanda wiggled and waved her arms. Her fat little legs churned. And then she burst into tears. Kate let her cry. There were so many children in various stages of distress that the noise of one more didn't matter, she decided.

He returned only minutes later with a huge bag of food—and a high chair into which he managed to stuff Amanda before filling her bottle from a carton of milk. "That should keep her busy long enough for us to eat."

Ben quickly devoured two hot dogs while Kate worked steadily on her hamburger. "It's wonderful," she admitted. "But then anything would taste good at this point."

While Ben patiently helped Amanda finish up his double order of fries, Kate perused the material from United Charities. "Brownley seemed like such a nice guy," she mused. "And UC has a great reputation. Still, he has a motive to want me out of the way."

"A little too dramatic, Kate. Just because he plays around doesn't mean he's a killer."

"I wish I'd had a chance to talk with him."

"You still may be able to, but he's not our only suspect." Ben grimaced at the word. "I'm beginning to sound like a cheap detective, but while I'm playing the role, let me suggest that there's still Hedrick."

"Which means you think Amanda is the key?"

"I don't know but I'd like to find out. Have you explored the possibility that Amanda might be an heiress?"

"An heiress?" she asked in surprise. "Where'd that come from?"

"Your cousins must have left some kind of estate. Maybe Hedrick wants to get his hands on it."

"There's a small amount of money in trust, but how would that benefit him?"

"Maybe there're other relatives you don't know about who might put in a claim for her. Hedrick could be working for them, trying to get Amanda away from you."

"Then why wouldn't they come forward or go to court?" she asked.

"I don't know, but I think we should explore every angle. If Amanda is the key to these attacks, the lawyer is our only lead in Denver. What did you think of him?''

"We never met. He sent me lots of paperwork, and we talked on the phone. But a social worker delivered Amanda.''

"Maybe you should meet the man. Could be something's going on about the adoption—'' Ben shook his head. "But, on the other hand, why would the guy want to kill you? Doesn't make sense.''

"You're suspicious, though, aren't you?''

Ben nodded.

"Why don't we check him out? Since this is all about adoptions and babies, we can pose as an an adoptive couple. Maybe he's running some kind of scam where he...'' Her voice trailed off.

"Kills the mother and kidnaps her baby? Pretty farfetched.'' Ben was intent on the problem. "I know that logically this is out of left field, but if there is a connection, I'd hate for us to turn our backs on it.''

"Then let's do it!'' Kate said. "We're so good at playing man and wife—'' she shot him a teasing look "—that we can try again as adoptive parents.''

"Hedrick's never seen you,'' Ben mused.

"Not unless he was the one who shot at me.''

"In which case he knows you're a redhead. You'll need some kind of disguise. A wig maybe.''

"You're kidding!''

"Not just for Hedrick, but for any time we're out in public. That hair of yours still shouts, Kate. It's impossible to bury it under a cap. The enemy is nameless and faceless so let's don't take any chances. You have Amanda to think about, too,'' he reminded her.

"Okay, I'll get a wig, but first let's see if Hedrick will give us an appointment. Oh, and I need someone to look after the baby. I wonder if I dare ask Tina again?''

''Promise her a bonus when all this is over,'' Ben suggested. He stood up and hoisted Amanda into his arms. ''Now let's hit the pay phones and start making calls.''

AN HOUR LATER, Kate passed a store window and a stranger stared back. Ben was right about the wig. If she didn't recognize herself, who else would? She fluffed out her blond curls and tilted her head to the side, studying her reflection.

Ben looked over at her with a grin. ''Glad you decided on the 'Bette Midler.' It's the very last look anyone would expect from you.''

''I really liked the 'Princess Di'—''

''Too sedate.''

''And the 'Ivana Trump' was a bit much.''

''The 'Dolly Parton' wasn't bad.''

''Too big. But I love these curls. Too bad you can't see Hedrick until tomorrow,'' she commented.

''I was lucky to get an appointment so quickly. His secretary softened at the word *adoption.* Said she'd work us in. It seems Hedrick has a tender spot for adoptive couples.''

''Don't you think that's significant?''

''It could be. Okay, Bette, let's get you a new wardrobe.''

The department stores were mobbed with shoppers taking advantage of pre-Christmas sales, filling the aisles and crowding the dressing rooms.

''I can't take this, Ben,'' Kate decided. ''Maybe I can cut my hair, wear the cap, roll up a pair of your jeans and pretend I'm a teenage boy.''

"A boy?" Ben shook his head. "Never. Let's look for a small boutique with nothing on sale."

"Where I'll pay a fortune."

"It's up to you, Kate. Crowded dressing room or big money."

"I've had all I can take. Let's go for the big-money chic boutique."

As it turned out, Shirl's Boutique wasn't all that expensive—and it certainly wasn't chic. But they were the only customers, and Shirl, a heavy woman dressed in black with an abundance of eye shadow, gave them a warm welcome.

"You just have a seat here," she advised, maneuvering Ben to a comfortable love seat and finding a baby-sitter for Amanda. "Carlene!" she called out. "Come and get this baby. You're not doing anything but watching TV. Give her some sherbet from the fridge back there. The baby can eat sherbet, can't she?"

Kate hesitated. Could she? She glanced at Ben, who nodded. "That would be fine, but I don't want to inconvenience—"

"Carlene's only watching a soap opera. It's no trouble, hon."

A skinny teenager appeared, sighing dramatically at the interruption. Seeing Amanda she brightened and held out her arms. The baby went to her without hesitation. Everyone seemed to have a better handle on what Amanda wanted than she, Kate thought as Carlene disappeared into the back with the happy baby.

"When a woman's shopping, she needs to concentrate and not worry about her kid. Now what can I do for you, honey?"

"I need a couple of outfits, one casual, one business, and everything that goes with them—from top to toe, inside and out."

"We'll start inside." Shirl decided, hauling out an armful of what was obviously her kind of lingerie—filmy, lacy and showy—and leading Kate to a dressing room.

To her surprise, Kate felt sensuous and a little erotic as she chose half a dozen pairs of high-cut bikini panties and two bras that were more lace than elastic. Not her thing at all, but what the hell, she decided. It was time for a new look. She might as well start at the skin.

After settling on a fleecy, navy-blue warm-up and a couple of turtle-necked sweaters, Kate returned to the dressing room with a few choices in the dress-for-success category, including a black pantsuit that she figured would be the one.

Until Shirl appeared in the doorway with a vivid green outfit. "Hon, this looks just like you. It'll be perfect with your hair, whatever the color," she added with a wink.

"You can tell it's—"

"Not your natural color, but it's lovely." She puffed up a little, proud of spotting a dye job. Kate kept her smile to herself. If Shirl only knew!

"Now try this on. It'll be sensational."

Obligingly, Kate slipped on the skirt and buttoned up the long jacket, which stopped just an inch short of the skirt's hemline. "I don't know...."

"A very popular look," Shirl assured her, "long jacket, short skirt—"

"Very short skirt," Kate said. "Too short."

"Hon, that's the style, and you've got great legs. Flaunt 'em."

"No, I—"

"Let's ask your husband. He'll agree."

"No, that's not necessary."

"Oh, I bet he's the kind who likes to keep his wife under wraps," Shirl said in a whisper.

"No, that's not it. I mean he's not like that." What in the world was she trying to say? He's not my husband! She kept her mouth shut.

"Then let's show him," the ebullient Shirl announced as she took firm hold of Kate's arm and led her from the dressing room. "Hey, hon, do you like your wife in this outfit?"

Ben was waiting on the sofa—keeping an eye on Amanda, who was busy smearing herself with sherbet in Shirl's small office—and listening to the women's conversation.

"We need a man's point of view," Shirl announced. "Now I don't want to prejudice your decision, but I have to tell you how much I like your wife in this outfit."

Ben stood up. "I'll be glad to cast my vote— whether with you or my wife...." Ben slowly walked around Kate, his eyes roaming her body. The color was terrific, an emerald green that brought out the lights in her eyes. He could only imagine how sensational the outfit would look with her wonderful *red* hair.

The jacket fit snugly over her round breasts and the skirt was short, very short, with a daring little kick pleat that caught his eye. He'd been right earlier. She would never be mistaken for a boy.

"I told Shirl the skirt was too short—"

Ben shook his head.

"The look too unprofessional—"

He disagreed again.

"It's not appropriate for the office, Ben."

"Why not?" he asked. "You look great." He let his eyes consume her once more, this time without the pressure of making a critical decision. Just looking. And enjoying. The remembrance of their kiss flashed into his mind. He'd done it to tease her, but he'd ended up surprising himself. The warmth of it still lingered.

He realized he was staring and quickly slipped back into his familiar teasing mode. "Especially with those boots. Short skirts and high-heeled boots—that's very sexy, darling."

Kate gave him a withering look.

"My wife will take it," he told Shirl with a smile that was all innocence.

"No, I—"

"It'll be great for the office party, darling," he continued, a devilish glint in his eyes.

"Two against one," Shirl said happily.

Kate fled to the dressing room. "No fair ganging up." She stripped off the suit and handed it to Shirl.

"Well?"

"Wrap it," she said. "Even though I'll be embarrassed to wear it. My thighs are so—"

"Your thighs are fine. What I wouldn't give for 'em. But if you're worried..." Shirl hurried out to return moments later with an armful of color—hot pink tights, striped leotard, even a matching headband.

"Workout clothes, all in your size. What do you think?"

"Wrap 'em," Kate said. "I even know of a spa where I can work out."

"I've got shoes, too, hon."

"Wrap 'em," Kate repeated.

"THAT WAS actually fun," she admitted two hours later as they dragged themselves to the car, loaded with clothes, toys and diapers for Amanda. "I can't believe I said that," she added. "I usually hate shopping. But the baby stuff was so cute. I understand why grandparents get hung up on buying for kids."

"Does Amanda have any grandparents?" Ben asked as he strapped the baby into her car seat.

Kate stopped to think. "I know Libby's parents aren't living, but I'm not sure about Derek's. I guess I should look into that. Anyway, no one stepped forward when I got custody. If there were relatives, and they'd wanted the baby, wouldn't they have just said so instead of trying to kill me?" she asked. "I wasn't exactly fighting for custody."

"That's true, but you never know how people think. There could be someone out there who's obsessed and doesn't know how to deal with it."

"Then we have a real problem, don't we?" Kate asked. "It's impossible to predict what a crazy person's going to do."

"If we can't predict it, there's nothing we can do about it," he said with what she thought was a kind of illogical logic. "So don't worry. Now, what's next on your agenda?"

"There's so much to think about. I wish we could just home in on one thing—like Brownley. If only he'd been at the mall."

"But he wasn't. You went back to the UC booth half a dozen times. Brownley was a no-show. So we move on to the car repair." He handed her the cellular phone. "Call the shop."

It was a frustrating call. "They haven't even gotten to my car. Can you believe that? Maybe this afternoon, they say. I won't hold my breath. But they tell me to call back at six."

"You could have it towed to another garage," he suggested.

"Where I'd have to start all over. No, let's leave it there and pick up a newspaper."

"A newspaper?" He looked over at her as he edged out of the parking lot.

"I have to find an apartment for me and Amanda."

"Hold off on that. You need wheels first."

"I guess." She leaned back in the car seat. "Maybe I'm just being a fool to worry. Maybe I should take Amanda and go home."

"You're not being foolish. It was just yesterday that someone shot at you—"

"Yesterday? It seems like years ago," Kate murmured in an exhausted voice. "It probably seems even longer to you. Sorry to tie up your life like this."

"Like I said, Kate, it's only been a day, and I didn't have anything better to do. There were no good ball games on TV," he added with a grin. "But we do need to hang out in Denver until your car's ready. Got any suggestions?"

"Well, I bought a new exercise outfit. . . ."

"Don't look at me."

"Are we anywhere near the Willowdale complex?"

"Not far. What does that have to do with exercise?"

"Sky-High Spa is located at Willowdale. I could go there, pretend to be checking it out for possible membership—and look for Coral. Or at least ask questions about her."

"What about your little friend?" He nodded toward the back seat. "What are your plans for Amanda?"

The baby was napping, lulled by the movement of the car.

"Oh, yes. Well...maybe I can take her with me. Some spas have nurseries...."

"Or you could check her with your coat," Ben commented.

"All right, all right. I know I'm not the world's best mom," she said, "but you have to remember that I'm new at all this."

"Understood," he said. "Just don't *forget* the baby!"

She scrunched down in the seat, somewhat diminished as he navigated the traffic. "Where are we going?"

"Where else? To the spa."

"But you...Amanda—"

"We'll hang out together. Maybe find a bar and watch a little wrestling."

"A bar? Wrestling? You can't—" She realized that he was putting her on. "Thanks, Ben," she said. "I really would like to see inside of Sky-High, and since we've got time to kill..."

"And since you need to work on your thighs."

Kate groaned. "Did you hear *everything* we said in the dressing room?"

"We Native Americans have ears like foxes, haven't you heard?"

WHILE BEN TOOK Amanda to Willowdale's skating rink, Kate grabbed her new workout clothes and headed for the spa.

On her only other visit she hadn't even been inside and had seen no employees except the janitor, so she wasn't prepared for the luxury that confronted her.

The lobby was beautifully decorated with photographic artwork adorning the walls. She crossed the highly polished floors on exotic colorful rugs to the reception desk.

"Hi, there!" called out a perky receptionist wearing Sky-High Spa's logo T-shirt and shorts.

"Hi, there," Kate returned. She hadn't meant to mock the girl, but it didn't matter, because the little blonde seemed totally oblivious.

"Ready to exercise?" she asked.

"Well, I'm just... I'm not a member," Kate said quickly. *Don't let anyone know why you're really here,* she warned herself.

"We can remedy that." She picked up a clipboard and pencil. "Name?"

Kate equivocated as she looked over the brochure. "Do you give tours?"

"We do better than that. Anytime between now and the new year, we'll give you three free sessions. Then, after the first of the year, you can make that big commitment."

"Hmm," Kate mumbled.

"Most people are waiting for January first to get into an exercise program. You'll be way ahead...."

Kate realized that this woman already had her signed up and working out. Well, what could it hurt? It would cost her nothing—and give her an opportunity to find out where in the world Coral had gotten to.

"Now, tell me, do you want to lose weight or tone up—or both?" She glanced at Kate with a look that implied she definitely needed both.

"Both, certainly," Kate agreed.

"That's the spirit. You won't be disappointed. Sky-High is the best. It costs a little more, but you'll see the difference when you join us. Your name?" she asked again.

"Kate—" She broke off, remembering Ben's warning as he let her out in front of the spa. *Keep a low profile. Don't advertise yourself.*

"Kaitlin."

"Mmm. Could you spell that, please?"

Kate did so, following with a last name plucked from the blue, or maybe, she thought, from the great outdoors. "Snow. That's S-N-O-E," she said.

Before she knew it, Kate was signed up, given a temporary ID card and a locker key and sent off toward the lounge.

She pushed through the brass-decorated double doors and entered a sitting room with sofas, coffee table, television and a sideboard containing herbal teas, decaffeinated coffee and a frosty pitcher of ice water filled with lemon slices.

"What have I gotten myself into?" she asked aloud.

At a counter in front of the lockers, workout clothes—T-shirts, shorts and socks—were neatly folded in front of a pretty young woman who asked, "Small, medium or large?"

"Umm, I have my own things. Is that all right?"

"Of course, but you'll need this." She handed Kate a fluffy white robe. "For later, when you finish your workout and want to enjoy our other amenities—the Jacuzzi, steam room and sauna."

"Oh, of course," Kate said, nodding her thanks.

"If you hurry, you'll make Jennifer's step class."

"Jennifer?"

"Jennifer Kersten, one of the managers."

Kate smiled her thanks. If anyone would know about Coral, the manager certainly would.

In her hot-pink tights and striped leotard, she joined the class beside a middle-aged woman who huffed and puffed her way through the warm-up. Kate put her step down beside the woman's. Theirs were the only single steps in the aerobic room, where everyone else had stacked two or three—even four.

Jennifer was tall, probably five foot ten, with short, blond-streaked hair and a well-muscled body that moved like a machine. Kate made it through the warm-up with her and then things got complicated.

"I've never been able to do these turns," she wheezed to her overweight neighbor, who agreed.

"Jennifer is...a...killer...isn't she?" The panting punctuated each word. "Even...tougher than...Mark."

"Who's Mark?" Kate asked.

"Her husband, the other manager," she said, panting but holding to the tempo. "You can't miss him—bald and hunky."

"Ladies in the back, keep moving," Jennifer called out.

Kate could feel perspiration pooling under her wig, which was going as limp as her muscles. Finally, Jennifer began the warm-down, slow, easy floor movements.

"I'm Edie," Kate's friend declared.

"Hi, I'm Kaitlin." She extended a damp hand.

"And I'm heading for the steam room and then the Jacuzzi. How about you?"

"In a little while," Kate replied. She wanted to find out about the managers, Mark and Jennifer. Were they the ones Coral wanted to replace? To learn more, Kate was going to have to hit the machines.

And were there ever machines—one, she figured, for all six hundred muscles in the body, plus bikes, cross-country skiers, stair climbers, treadmills and some weird things Kate couldn't identify, like a glassy-smooth pad designed for sliding on in quilted shoes, an exercise that had to be coordinated perfectly. Kate stayed away from it as she took her seat on an easy-looking leg lift machine.

"How's it going?" a voice asked in a silky caressing tone.

"Umm. Fine."

The voice belonged to a lanky, muscled young man, just under six feet with shoulder-length blond hair. Definitely not Mark. He was tanned and sleek, as if he'd just been oiled. His features were delicate, and his pale blue eyes didn't meet hers directly. The look was one that women at the spa probably found devastatingly attractive.

But not Kate. She thought about Ben and his strong, chiseled features, his dark piercing eyes and his roguish look that appreciated her so thoroughly, unlike this young man's clinical appraisal. He seemed to weigh each muscle and molecule and find what was missing. "New to the spa?" he asked.

She nodded. "I'm Kaitlin."

"I'm Dylan. Let me take you through the routine."

She managed to make small talk and listen to his appraisal of her body before she asked her first question. "Have you worked here long, Dylan?"

"Long enough." He counted her leg lifts. "Eight, nine, ten. Two more, eleven, twelve. Good job. Now let's work on those pecs."

*Okay,* Kate thought. *He's not taking that bait. I'll go another way.* She followed him to the next machine. "Is the owner around today?"

He lowered the bar and waited for her to sit down. "This is the triceps press. It'll work the pectoralis group. Do you know Coral?"

"Nope. I've just heard of her. I thought she might be here tonight, one of those hands-on types." Kate looked around.

He shook his head, barely disturbing his blond tresses. "That's Mark's job. She stays behind the scenes."

"Where is she—on vacation?"

"I guess." Dylan set the weight. "Start low on this press. Twenty pounds. She's gone on a cruise, or so Mark says. Sort of unexpected. She left him a note."

Kate tried to find out more as she moved on to a lower-body machine where she managed to do a series of fifteen reps on sixty pounds. "I don't believe it," she gasped.

"Strong thighs," Dylan commented disinterestedly.

Her routine completed, Kate was still short on information. "I'm hoping to join in January—if I can handle the fees, not to mention the regime," she told Dylan. "It's so luxurious here, I doubt I'll be able to resist. Do you think Coral will be back by the first of the year?"

Dylan shrugged. "You'll have to ask Mark." He handed Kate a towel. "Try the Jacuzzi. It'll help those muscles." With a smile of sorts, he was gone.

Well, just a quick dip, she told herself when she reached the most provocative section of the lounge— the hot tub, sauna and steam room and behind them a row of showers that were as beautifully appointed as the spa's reception area, all elegance with mahogany and brass fittings.

She sank into the Jacuzzi just as Edie appeared, wrapped in a big towel. "Don't forget the cucumbers," she advised.

"What?" Kate asked.

"Here." She reached into a glass container and handed Kate two slices of cucumber and an icy-cold washcloth, folded lengthwise. "Close your eyes, plop the cukes on your lids and the cloth on top. Heaven," she said, shedding her robe and sinking into the tub beside Kate.

Kate agreed. "Especially on this overworked body. Every muscle is quivering."

Edie smirked. "Dylan has that effect on people."

Kate agreed halfheartedly. "He's attractive."

"So says every woman here. They're all wild for him." She lowered her voice. "Even the owner."

"Coral Lampiere? Really?" Kate leaned as close to Edie as the jets would allow. "Sounds like a romance."

"Who knows? But Coral usually stayed close to him. I was surprised when she went on that cruise alone—"

"Oh, the cruise—she told you about that . . . ?"

"Well, no. She never mentioned it. I think Jennifer told me. No, maybe it was Mark. He's a little jealous of Dylan, you know. Course, you can't blame him. Mark used to be the sex symbol around here with his strong-as-an-ox physique. Then along came Dylan...."

Kate definitely needed to see Mark for herself. Eventually. Meanwhile, she was too relaxed, too... Suddenly, she sat up. She'd forgotten all about Amanda! Ben would have every right to be upset with her; she wasn't a very good mother. Making her apologies to Edie, she removed the cucumber slices and stood up. A quick shower—careful of the wig, she reminded herself—and then she needed to get dressed and get out of there.

On her way out, she spotted Jennifer and the man she was quickly able to ID as Mark, her husband. He was an inch or two under six feet with a bull-like body, tapering muscles and very bald head.

He stepped forward, hand extended. "A new face. Enjoy your workout?"

"Loved it," Kate lied. "Can't wait to come back."

"Great. I'll be looking for you. I'm Mark Kersten, Sky-High's manager."

Kate noticed a slight narrowing of Jennifer's eyes at that. Two managers. A power struggle, maybe?

"I'm Kaitlin."

Jennifer stepped forward, friendly but somehow in charge. "How was the aerobics class?"

"I coped," Kate said.

"Come back soon. We're open every day, from 6:00 a.m. till 9:00 p.m."

"Thanks, I will." As she pushed through the door, she almost collided with a woman coming into the spa. Kate waited a beat and then retraced her steps, stopping at the desk. "I'm sure I know the woman who just walked in," she said, "but I can't think of her name."

"Oh, that's Paige Norcross."

"Thank you. Now I remember." *Do I ever,* she said to herself.

# Chapter Six

The wind whipped off the mountain and over the plain, creating a tunnel between the spa and the hotel across the courtyard. Kate held on to her wig with both hands and hurried toward the ice rink. Her heart pounded with excitement. Wait until Ben heard what she'd found out.

Two lonely skaters circled the dime-size rink. No Ben. No Amanda. Irrational ideas hurtled through her mind.

Something had happened to Ben and Amanda! Her attacker had returned and gone after them. Kidnapped, even murdered—

She stopped and took a deep breath. "Get a grip, Kate," she ordered herself. The past twenty-four hours had taken their toll, causing her to find sinister schemes everywhere, even here at a skating rink where Ben and Amanda had probably gotten bored, certainly gotten cold and decided to go inside. The hotel was the obvious choice. She headed for it.

Small and commercial, it was decorated in a Western motif, or what some decorator decided was Western when he lined the lobby with faux leather chairs in the shape of saddles. On one side was a bar where a

few patrons watched TV at tables that appeared to be
made of cattle troughs. Stuffed buffalo heads,
Christmas bows around their horns, looked down
mournfully from the wall. But they weren't looking at
Ben and Amanda. Those two weren't among the bar's
patrons.

The other side of the lobby continued the Western
theme with antlers hung on the wall above the sheepskin chairs and love seats. "Ugh," Kate said, turning
to leave and then seeing two young and attractive
women standing near one of the chairs, laughing and
chatting with someone she couldn't see. They were
waitresses, she assumed from their outfits of fringed
shirts, short skirts and cowboy boots. Noticing their
flirtatious mood, Kate could guess whom they might
be talking to. Then she heard a delighted gurgle of
laughter.

Amanda.

"This is absolutely the best baby..." one of the
women was saying. Her long dark hair was worn in a
braid, and her dark eyes sparkled.

As Kate made her way around the circle of furni-
ture she saw that the sparkle wasn't directed toward
Amanda, who was sitting on the floor, chewing happily on a soda cracker, but toward Ben, looking comfortable in the sheepskin chair.

"You're great with her, a natural," Ben said.

"I'd love to baby-sit sometime," the other waitress
spoke up, in a smooth, silky voice.

Kate decided it was time to intervene. "*Darling,*
there you are," she said mischievously, approaching
Ben. Her arrival seemed to take them all by surprise.

Amanda chortled, "Ma-ma," and crunched another handful of crackers.

Ben looked up lazily from the chair, a soft drink in his hand. *"Sweetheart,"* he said, gently mocking, "you took so long that I almost gave up. Then I found the hotel, where these lovely ladies came to my rescue."

The sparkling waitress kept the sparkle going. "We've enjoyed every minute. It was a boring afternoon, anyway, and Ben and Amanda livened things up."

Kate reached for Amanda's snowsuit on the back of a chair. "They have a way of doing that, don't they?" She began to push and pull Amanda's pliant body into the garment, coloring a little under the watchful eyes of the two women.

"I could do that," the braided waitress offered.

"I'll manage, thanks," Kate replied, trying to soften her words with a smile. She ought to have been glad the women were interested in Amanda. Except she knew it wasn't the baby who'd held their interest. It was long-legged, broad-shouldered, dark-eyed, sexy Ben, who stood up lazily, a smile on his wide sensuous mouth.

He put a large bill beside his tab. "You ladies have been great. I'm very appreciative."

"Thanks, Ben," they said in unison. "Come back real soon." They drifted away, heads close together. Kate was sure they were talking about her.

"Sorry I took so long, but—"

Ben picked up Amanda. "I expected it," he said philosophically. "Mandy and I had fun at the rink, but it got damned cold. The hotel was a nice oasis."

"You certainly looked comfortable. I guess a cute baby makes it easy to attract women." As soon as the words were out, Kate wished she hadn't said them. It was absurd for her to make any kind of comment on Ben's relations with women.

But he didn't seem affected as he said with a cocky grin, "Matter of fact, I never found it difficult—even without a baby around." He glanced over at her as they walked through the lobby. "And you've got to admit, I had the baby around for quite a while today."

"I know, I know. A real mother would be more thoughtful. But I was enjoying the luxury of the spa for a moment there. As it turned out, I'm glad I stayed as long as I did. You won't believe what happened." They were outside again in the cold, heads low, making their way toward the car.

"You found your missing friend and caught up on old times."

"Nope. Not a sign of Coral, but on my way out, I saw Paige Norcross!"

"That's great. Who's Paige Norcross?"

"The 'other woman,' the one who was with Robert Brownley at his house that night!"

As THEY DROVE through the rush-hour traffic, Kate pulled off the wig and shook her hair free. "I couldn't believe it, Ben. Brownley's mistress, girlfriend, whatever, right there in the spa. It was—" She broke off as they turned onto the expressway. "Wait, stop. I've got to call about my car."

"I already did."

She looked over at him.

"Called from the hotel. The car's still not ready."

She breathed a sigh, unable to keep the relief out of her voice. "Then I don't guess Amanda and I can look for another place to stay tonight."

"Guess not."

He spoke the words nonchalantly, but Kate could have sworn she saw the hint of a smile on his lips. Of course, she might have imagined it. But she didn't imagine her own excitement. She was going home with Ben again, and she liked the idea. She studied his chiseled profile, wondering what he was thinking. Was he glad, too?

He turned to look at her. "We need to stop for groceries."

Oh, well, Kate thought. At least she knew what was on his mind. She was thinking about going home with him; he was thinking about food!

"Does Mandy like anything special?" he asked.

Not yet really sure of the baby's tastes, Kate tried to fake it. "Umm. She likes milk—and juice. And, you know, baby food. Oh!" Kate remembered, "she doesn't like carrots, but I haven't noticed any particular favorites. Nothing is easy to feed her!"

Ben laughed out loud. "You've got a lot to learn about this kid."

"I know," she said seriously, "and I'm trying, Ben."

"You'll get there."

"Thanks," she said softly. "For everything."

He shrugged. "It's been fun." And then he realized it really had been.

They hit the grocery store on the run, moving up and down the aisles and grabbing jars, cans, bags of fruit and vegetables, and were soon on their way up the narrow winding road to his house. Night had fallen, but this time the dark wasn't frightening to Kate. It seemed to wrap them all in a veil of secrecy and safety.

Kate carried Amanda inside as Ben unloaded the groceries. "I can't wait for you to hack into Paige Norcross's life," she said. "Then we'll have some answers. You can get to it right away," she said confidently and, as it turned out, optimistically.

They'd had to unpack. Fix dinner. Amuse Amanda. After dinner, there was washing up to do—the dishes and the baby. When Kate finally went upstairs to take a shower, shampoo and blow-dry her wig-flattened hair and get Amanda ready for bed, two hours had passed.

And all the while she hadn't even thought about Paige, the spa or Robert Brownley. As she'd watched Ben in the kitchen, chopping peppers and celery for stir-fry, his big strong hands moving more expertly than she could have imagined, she'd been mesmerized. Even as she shook off the glow Ben created, she was aware of something else—how much like a family they suddenly seemed.

The thought filled her with emotions that she tried to back away from. She should be worrying about the person who shot at her, searching for an answer to the mystery so she could get back to her apartment—and her life.

She wasn't supposed to be enveloped in this blanket of satisfaction, basking in it and glowing with pleasure at how satisfying it was to be in Ben Blackeagle's home again, sharing the evening with him.

When she got into her new warm-up and came downstairs after Amanda had fallen asleep, Ben was finally at his computer. But he looked puzzled. "Are you sure this woman's name is Paige Norcross?"

"Positive."

"Well, there's no such person. At least I can't find any trace of her. No driver's license, phone listing, credit rating. Nothing."

Kate sank down on the sofa. "I was sure if anybody could find her, you could."

Ben got up and stretched. "And you're right. I could. *If* she existed. The name is an alias, Kate. Possibly the kind that prostitutes use."

Kate sat up straight on the sofa. "That fits, doesn't it! She's not just a girlfriend, she's a—"

"Hooker," he finished.

She sank back on the sofa. "Why not! There's no reason Brownley's lover has to be an amateur. He might prefer professionals. In many ways, that's more discreet. But it gives him just as much reason to come after me and keep me quiet. A prostitute in his own house while his wife is away! I need to call him, confront him with this—"

"If he's a threat, that could be dangerous. Remember my advice—don't tell a suspect you're on to him! We'll have to consider the next move carefully. But not tonight," he added softly.

"No, not tonight," she repeated as he handed her a snifter of brandy. She took a sip. "It gets more and more complex, doesn't it?"

"Life is that way, Kate." He nodded toward the phone. "Not the time for calls, but you should pick up your messages from the office. There're a couple on the machine."

She went to the phone and hit the button on the answering machine. There were two messages from Tina about office business and one from the garage about deducting charges from her bill because of the delay.

She looked at Ben pointedly. "You must have put the fear of God in them."

"Let's just say they understood my displeasure with the way they'd treated you."

She smiled her thanks. "I'd better check my messages at home while I'm still in the business mode." Not quite sure what that meant, Kate dialed her home phone number. "Maybe some of the baby-sitting services have called back."

Two had; neither could offer any help. There were several other calls, none important. And then there was a last message, muffled, barely discernible. *"Kate McNair, you think you're safe, but you're not. I'm coming for you."*

"Oh, God," Kate said, her hand trembling so violently that the brandy spilled down the front of her warm-up jacket. The nightmare wasn't over.

BEN MADE a taped copy of the message for the police. "Though I doubt if they can do much with voice tracing or matching from this, Kate. So don't get your hopes up. I can't even tell if it's the voice of a man or a woman."

"But if they could get a sample of Brownley's voice—"

"No, Kate. There's nothing to lead them to Brownley, only speculation. They have no authority to tape him."

"I'm just trying to make some sense out of this. The attacks and threats—"

He sat beside her on the sofa, and she was glad of his presence. She could feel his warmth, his strength; it made *her* strong. But even Ben couldn't stop the crazy careening rush toward—whatever was happening to her.

"This is getting worse, isn't it?"

His look seemed stern but his voice was comforting. "It's going to be all right. We'll get to the bottom of this." He put his arm around her. It was such a casual gesture that for a moment she hardly noticed.

"Thanks for not letting me go back to my apartment. I couldn't have handled this alone." Suddenly she was overwhelmingly aware of his touch, firm on her shoulder. "But we can't keep imposing on you." Her voice was unsteady.

"Don't worry about that now. We're doing okay. In fact, we sometimes even make a pretty good team."

"Like tonight," she said.

He looked at her questioningly.

"Not a detective team," she added, "but together, cooking dinner, putting Mandy to bed. We were like a family," she added without thinking. Then she blushed and looked away again. She hadn't meant to group them that way. Besides, what did she even know about family, really? She bit her lip and looked toward the fire. "If I'd ever had a family..."

"Everyone has a family, Kate." He was curious about her remark and the intensity with which she'd made it.

"Except me. Oh, I had a mother and father, but we weren't any kind of unit. There were nannies from the time I could remember."

"You said your father was in the foreign service."

"Yes, we lived all over the world when I was small. I was mostly alone. Except for the nannies. They were always there."

"What about your mother? She didn't work, did she?"

"Not in the conventional sense, but she was my father's hostess, assistant, his right arm. They were a closed corporation, very much in love and totally dependent on each other."

Ben got the picture. Two strong adults, heavily bonded. A little girl on the outside. "Still, traveling around the world must have been quite an education for you."

"When I was about ten, they sent me away to private school, first in England, then in Switzerland. I did all my traveling when I visited my parents on holidays, but I don't remember much about that." She laughed ruefully. "Poor little rich girl, you're thinking. Only we weren't all that rich."

Ben wasn't sure what to say. "I guess it was a lonely time for you," he managed, aware of a whole new side of Kate, one that surprised and touched him.

"Sometimes. When I got to junior high, my parents were on home leave. They let me finish high school in the States. I had good friends who often invited me home. And there was Carol. I mean, Coral."

"The woman who owns the spa? The one you're looking for?"

"Yes. She was the dance teacher at Edgemont School in Virginia. I think she knew how much I needed an adult's approval, and she was very sweet and kind to me."

"I bet you were a good dancer."

She laughed. "That's how much you know. I was awful. Scarcely knew my left foot from my right and had no sense of rhythm. But Carol was really encouraging. She used to take groups of us into Richmond to the ballet, and her classes made me feel special, even graceful—which I certainly wasn't. That's why I was excited about her being in Denver. Only now I can't find her."

"She's on a cruise. Cruises end."

"The whole vacation thing doesn't sound like Coral. I have a bad feeling about it and the spa—"

"Yet you want to go back."

When she nodded enthusiastically, Ben laughed. "You're amazing, Kate. You want something, you go after it. I've never known anyone so tenacious."

"I guess I had to be—to survive."

As she ran her fingers distractedly through her shiny clean hair, he noticed how it glittered and gleamed in the firelight. He had a sudden urge to gather the bright red tresses in his hands, bury his face in their fragrant brilliance. Instead, he took a deep breath, got to his feet and walked over to the fireplace.

"Okay," she said, her voice lightened up. "I've bared my soul. What about you?"

"Big family, lots of sibs. You know all that."

"No, I don't, not really," she countered. "Tell me. I want specifics."

"Okay. Here're the stats—three younger sisters, two of them married, one in college in Idaho. My baby brother's in film school in L.A."

"Your parents?"

"My mother died two years ago." He paused for a brief instant. "Dad died when I was thirteen."

"You were the man in the family," Kate said softly. "No wonder you know so much about children. I bet you reared your brother and sisters."

"My mom worked so I spent most of my young life going to school and baby-sitting. You might say I became an unwilling expert."

"An expert, just the same, especially compared to me. Like most only children I know nothing about *children!* Look at how inept I am with Amanda." Kate sighed. "It's obvious that I'm not a good parent. I wonder if I ever will be?"

"Just takes practice," he reminded her.

"Like changing diapers? I've practiced a hundred times and still can't get it right." She shook her head helplessly. "And I haven't given her much in the way of family life."

"There hasn't been time for that, Kate. Once you get your life straightened out, everything will be different."

"If that ever happens."

"We've still got plenty of clues to check out. There's lawyer Hedrick, Brownley and the elusive Paige Norcross, the mystery of your friend Coral...."

"The puzzle gets more and more complex—and dangerous," Kate said. "I'd think you would be tired of it by now."

"I told you, Kate—I love a good hunt."

His words triggered an image in her imagination. "Do you ever wear buckskins?"

"Buckskins? You mean as in cowboy-and-Indian movies?" Ben laughed. "You're a little off base, Kate. My Native American upbringing was on a reservation. The word conjures up tepees and buffalo to some people when it should bring to mind pickup trucks and convenience stores. Nope," he assured her, "I've never worn buckskins."

Embarrassed by what she was afraid he considered her stupid question, Kate tried to explain. "I was thinking about you hunting, with a bow and arrow, tracking wild animals...." She couldn't prevent a fantasy from flashing in her mind, Ben in buckskin, his chest bare. At the image, she felt her cheeks grow warm. "I know it's ridiculous—"

"Not altogether," he told her. "I actually have hunted with a bow and arrow."

"Really?" She felt vindicated.

"My Cheyenne grandfather used to take me up into the mountains. He was an expert tracker. He could read the trail of any animal—deer, wolf, bear—and birds like quail and pheasant. He showed me how to fit the pieces together—the broken twig, scratches on the bark of a tree, a half-faded track. It was his influence that led me into computers."

"How? That seems a funny connection."

"Using a computer is little more than tracking information, solving puzzles, following trails. It all seems very natural to me."

"You love your job, don't you?"

"I love my life, Kate," he said fervently. "Now that all the members of my family are on their own, taking care of themselves, I'm only responsible for me. I can do whatever I want to, all the things I missed along the way. I may sound self-indulgent, but I've earned everything I have and don't intend to ever give it up." He stretched his arms high over his head, flexing his shoulders. "It's a great life."

Kate suddenly felt very sad. Clearly, Ben had staked out his territory. He knew exactly where his life was going. And of course, if she had any indication that it was going her way, his statement convinced her otherwise. As for Kate's life, she didn't know what was happening.

She got up from the sofa. "I guess I should turn in, get rested up for whatever lies ahead tomorrow. And who knows what that will be," she added.

He held out a reassuring hand. "It'll be all right, Kate. Somehow, all of this will sort itself out."

His touch was warm; no, more than warm. It was electrifying. She started to pull away from his grasp, but then she stopped herself. She didn't want to lose the contact with him. She held on and wrapped her fingers around the hardness of his palm.

He rubbed his thumb comfortingly across the back of her hand. The sensation traveled along her nerve endings and lodged somewhere deep inside her. The firelight turned his skin to bronze and his eyes to dark pools of night. She couldn't stop looking at him.

With his other hand, he touched her face, tracing the line from her cheekbone to her chin. "I'm glad we talked tonight," he said. "I think I understand you more now."

She still couldn't take her eyes off his face. It mesmerized her and caused her heart to pound, her mouth to become dry. She wet her lips and tried to catch her breath. Then he slipped his hand into her hair and all of her determination faded away with the touch. She closed her eyes and emitted a soft moan.

"I love your hair," he said softly. "It reminds me of fire." He pulled her close. "I want to kiss you again, Kate. This time a real kiss, for us alone."

"Yes," she murmured in a voice that was strangled, husky. She raised her lips to his. Never had she wanted a kiss so much.

And never had a kiss so completely lived up to expectations! His mouth was warm and enveloping, his taste a faint mixture of coffee and brandy. Her reaction was spontaneous. She slipped her arms around his neck and pressed close, her breasts crushed against his broad chest, her hips fitting into his.

He wrapped his hands in her hair and cupped her head in his broad grasp. She felt him enveloping her completely as he pulled her close and their bodies meshed. She melted inside, her body turning liquid under his touch. As she parted her lips, she felt his tongue mate with hers, and a shiver ran along her skin.

Ben felt the tremor and responded to it. Her hair was molten silk beneath his fingers, her mouth a hot flame against his, and her body yielded to him, pressed against him. He almost lost himself in her curves and softness. Something inside told him that he should stop kissing her. But he didn't.

She was exciting and sensual as she trembled in his arms, open and vulnerable. He could feel the erratic pounding of her heart against his chest, the touch of her tongue on his. He slid his hand to her waist and then up, under her shirt. Her skin was soft and satiny. As he felt the curve of her breast, desire surged through him, hot and heavy. One more touch, he decided, one more kiss.

But then he stopped himself. He'd gone too far. Things had gotten too complicated; the situation was out of control. How had that happened? He'd brought Kate and Mandy into his home for one purpose only—to help them out.

But as he touched her, held her, kissed her, he knew he was about to get involved, really involved, and that wasn't what he'd intended.

Ben pulled his lips away from hers, still holding her in his arms. Her eyes were deep and questioning, her mouth soft and vulnerable. He took a long breath and tried to clear his head. "Quite a good-night kiss." He forced a lightness into his voice that he didn't feel and smiled down at her, trying to appear casual.

Her voice trembled an answer. "I didn't mean to..."

"I guess the tension got to both of us," he said, dropping his arms and turning away to stare into the fire's flickering depths.

"I think I'll go to bed now," she said in a quiet voice.

He stood unmoving. "Yeah, we both need a good night's rest."

Only as she started toward the stairs did he turn and look at her. The sight was compelling, her slim body that he'd so recently held in his arms, moving away from him. He wanted to ask her to come back, but he stopped himself.

She climbed the stairs, and then he called to her, but not to bring her back, just to give her comfort and reassurance. "Sleep well, Kate."

"I will," she replied. "I'm exhausted." She hurried up the stairs.

BUT SLEEP wouldn't come. Her mind was racing with the remembrance of Ben's touch on her skin and his mouth on hers. Her body ached with unfulfilled longings and needs. She turned on her side and clutched her pillow close, wishing it were Ben and knowing how foolish her fantasy was. But that didn't prevent it from invading her mind again. She hadn't wanted him to stop. She'd wanted the kiss to go on. Foolish, she told herself. And dangerous.

Kate groaned and covered her head with the pillow. What in the world was going on? She was acting like a woman in...what? In love! She cringed at the thought that those feelings might have been apparent to Ben. God, she hoped not, because she knew how he felt about her.

Hadn't he made it clear when they talked that he wanted no commitments? He'd raised one family; he didn't want another. Especially, she imagined, a woman with her life out of control.

Involvement with Ben would mean a quick affair. Nothing more. She couldn't fall in love with him. It would be foolish. Dangerous.

BEN WAS HAVING trouble falling asleep. The futon had become increasingly uncomfortable as the night wore on. At some point he'd moved to the sofa, and there he stared into the dying embers of the fire, thinking. He was supposed to take care of Kate, to give her temporary refuge until her life straightened out. That had been the deal. That had been all.

He sat up and ran his hands through his long hair. He hadn't expected there would be more to it. But from the very first day he'd been intrigued by her mixture of vulnerability and toughness.

He got out of bed, stumbled to the liquor cabinet where he poured a dram of brandy into a glass. He warmed it in his hands, thinking of that kiss that he'd broken off. He'd wanted her then, but he had known better than to go that final step.

That hadn't stopped the wanting. Right now he longed to feel her body next to his, to make love to her, to give her pleasure and delight.

And that was crazy. She had a business to run and a kid to take care of which didn't add up to his kind of woman! What was the matter with him? He downed the brandy. "Get a grip, Blackeagle," he muttered. "When was the last time you lost sleep over a woman?"

He couldn't remember. When he was fifteen, maybe? But here it was, two in the morning, and he couldn't sleep! There was no doubt that she was getting to him. In subtle ways she wasn't even aware of. The conversation about her family. The look of pain in her green eyes. The way her hair fell around her face and gleamed in the firelight. How her body felt against his.

He remembered that body—and how he'd pulled away from her. For a moment there, he'd almost taken her to bed. It had been difficult not to, but the complexity of their situation had stopped him. Trying not to be sorry that things had ended that way, he put down the glass with a thud.

There was one way to solve the problem of Kate McNair. It was simple. Once he found out who was stalking her, she and Amanda would go home, and he would put the sweetness of her mouth and the warmth of her body out of his mind.

Having made that decision, he climbed back onto the sofa. But it was a long time before he fell asleep.

# Chapter Seven

"I hope this isn't a wild-goose chase," Kate commented. Fighting early-morning traffic, they were on their way to the ESS office to meet Tina. "Maybe we should be after the surreptitious lovers, Paige Norcross and Brownley. They're the villains."

"We're not *after* anyone. We're trying to track down clues and see where they lead us. That means *all* clues, and Hedrick is our only Denver link to Amanda, and we happen to be in Denver, so—"

"And what about the spa? I should go there. Maybe get into their records..."

Ben was laughing now. "Ms. Sherlock Holmes! How do you intend to 'get into their records'?"

"I don't know, I..."

"Then let's go on with the plan. We'll visit Hedrick as prospective parents," Ben said. "If he seems clean, then we can take the next step. But since we've already set this up—"

"Why not, huh? Okay. You're right." Ben's theory was as valid as any other. Besides, so far neither one of them had the first shred of evidence for *any* of their theories.

They drove the rest of the way in silence, a continuation of the silence that had set their morning mood. Ben had been as quiet as Kate as they'd rushed around in his mountain house, drinking coffee and getting dressed. Kate had felt groggy and out of sorts, and Amanda, who'd awakened cheerfully, soon picked up on Kate's mood. Breakfast had been a series of "no's," spilled food and jangled nerves.

Through it all Ben was cool and calm, evincing nothing of what had passed between them the night before.

What really *had* gone on? Kate couldn't be sure. Maybe the sensuous closeness, the heat had been in her mind. For a moment, she'd thought he shared her feelings; now she wasn't sure. In fact, his silence in the morning and his present joking mood were an indication that he'd forgotten—or wanted to forget—what had happened.

They pulled into a no-parking zone in front of Kate's office building. "We'll only be inside a minute," Ben said, as he unloaded Amanda's stroller. With Ben bringing the baby equipment and Kate carrying the baby, they stepped off the elevator to be met by a distraught Tina.

"I've been calling and calling you—"

"Don't you have my car phone number?" Ben asked.

"No, but I'll be sure to have it from now on!"

"What's the matter?" Kate asked.

"This." Tina pointed dramatically at the door to the office. "Someone tried to break in. Look at the lock. See how the wood around it is gouged out?"

"Did they get in?" Kate asked. "Was anything taken?"

"No, either someone scared the would-be burglar away or he realized the lock was too strong to jimmy."

"Did you call the police?" Ben asked.

"They just left. Took all the information, but had no advice except to put an alarm system on the door and windows. They said it looked like an amateur job."

Ben and Kate glanced at each other. Kate swallowed hard, thinking about the threatening message on her answering machine. And now this. "Why would someone break into my office? There're nothing but ESS files inside."

"Maybe just another warning," Ben said grimly. "Tina and Amanda can't stay here," he added.

"You're right about that," her assistant responded. "No way. I want to go home. I'll baby-sit Amanda there." Then for the first time she seemed to notice Kate's appearance. "Blond hair? And a new suit? What's going on?"

"We'll explain at your place. Come on," Ben urged. "I want all three of you ladies out of here fast."

SHE WELCOMED THEM into her tiny apartment, which was as bright and airy as Tina herself, with piles of magazines on a low coffee table and pictures of her family scattered on top of the desk and bookcases. The walls were crammed with artwork; the sofa was piled with colorful pillows. This was a real home, Kate thought, comparing it to her own apartment, a place she'd barely settled into.

Amanda's eyes were drawn to a cluster of animal prints on the wall. She waved her arms and kicked, begging to get at them. To distract her, Kate settled the baby among the bright comfortable sofa pillows.

"God, I need an aspirin and a glass of wine—" Tina shot a glance at Kate. "Okay, no wine until you two get back. Now tell me more about this scheme of yours."

"There's a chance that these attacks on Kate might somehow be connected to Amanda, and if so the only link we have is the lawyer, Daniel Hedrick, who handles adoptions," Ben explained.

"So you two are playing an adoptive couple?"

"I know it's a long shot," Kate said, "but it is one way to get to the man and feel him out."

"You think he's running some sort of black-market baby scam?" Tina grinned. "I've seen this plot on TV a million times."

Ben looked at Kate and shrugged. "Maybe not that blatant, Tina, but you're on the right track. My plan is a simple one—to find out if Hedrick can profit from getting his hands on Mandy."

"And if he *can,* he'll probably want to sell Amanda to the highest bidder." At Kate's look of surprise, she went on. "Hey, stranger things have happened. Some people will do anything for a baby, steal them right out of the hospital nursery, kidnap them from grocery carts—"

"Tina, nothing that dramatic could be happening to us," Kate said, trying to stem the flow of terrible possibilities.

"Snatch them off the school playground..." Tina added, undaunted, as Amanda tired of the pillows and began to yell. "Just read the newspapers. Did you hear about the woman who was killed so someone could kidnap her baby?"

"Tina—" Kate glanced at Ben as she picked up the baby. "It's all too improbable...."

"I don't blame you for checking it out," Tina told Ben. "This Hedrick guy knows Kate is a single mom. With her gone, he could dummy up some court papers and grab Amanda and place her with anyone."

"I doubt if he'd risk his career to steal a baby," Ben commented dryly. "But there may be relatives, who want to avoid the courts. All of this is speculation, of course. We're still looking for facts."

"Facts! Use your imagination," Tina countered. "Mr. Big would send a flunky, use another name, stay in the background. The brains behind the scene. Don't you ever watch TV?" Her dark eyes gleamed, "Oh, I wish I could be in on it. I love to act, although I have to admit that you two look the part, well-to-do, good-looking. That color suits you, boss, and the short skirt is fabulous." Her eyes flicked over to Ben. "And you look pretty handsome, yourself, Mr. Blackeagle."

Ben wore a charcoal-gray suit, pale blue shirt and black string tie, his ponytail pulled back neatly at the nape of his neck. Tina was right, Kate thought, he looked wonderful.

"Amazing what a good suit can do," he quipped. "Come on, Kate, we've got to move. We're running late as it is and we need to stop by the police station and drop off this tape."

"Police again? What is it with you two? Tell me!" Then she threw up her hands in dismissal. "No, don't. I'm scared enough already."

"I wonder if we should leave Tina and Amanda alone?" Kate asked anxiously.

"I'm going to double-lock the door and put a chair under it. My windows have bars, and I'm two stories up. No, I feel safe here." She shivered a little. "But that office—"

"I'll take care of the office later," Ben told her.

"Promise you'll hurry back."

"We will," Kate said. "And thanks, Tina. You're wonderful."

"Just remember that at Christmas bonus time, please!"

BEN SAT in Daniel Hedrick's waiting room, thumbing through a magazine and listening to Kate talk with Hedrick's secretary. She was laying it on too thickly, but what could he do? She was clearly beyond reining in.

"I love children," Kate bubbled. "I'd like at least four. So would Ben. When we were dating, we talked about having a family. Now that we're married, it seems time, but—"

Out of the corner of his eye, he saw Kate's eyes well with tears. Kim, Hedrick's secretary, was quick with a tissue.

"Thank you," Kate said, sniffing.

"Do you mind if I ask about your problem, Mrs. Black?" Kim inquired in a near-whisper, even though there was no one else in the waiting room.

Kate nodded. "I can't seem to get pregnant although we've tried everything. I can't tell you how many times I've taken my temperature during my fertile time—you know," she said confidentially, in a lowered voice. "Poor Ben. I call him home from work in the middle of the day, and he has to perform on cue."

She smiled toward Ben, who was beginning to get very uncomfortable but couldn't do anything to stop this spiel for fear of negating the whole process.

"He does wonderfully," she assured Kim, who nodded knowingly and glanced at Ben through lowered lashes. "But so far—nothing. We even tried artificial insemination—"

Her story was interrupted by a buzz from the inner office. Ben breathed a sigh of relief as Kim announced, "Mr. Hedrick can see you now."

DANIEL HEDRICK was cool. Not crook cool or gangster cool, but pale and watchfully cool. He was unimpressively small, with a neat compact body, an impeccably tailored suit and perfectly coiffed brown-gray hair. His forehead was high and gave him an intelligent look. His eyes were blue and watchful. Ben decided immediately that he was a good lawyer, tough but smooth enough to keep his opponent off guard.

He settled Ben and Kate in large comfortable chairs and poured each of them a cup of coffee from a silver service on the sideboard before looking directly at them with his clear, penetrating eyes.

"Tell me about your plans to adopt a baby," he said, positioning a legal pad in front of him on the desk and picking up a silver pen.

Kate couldn't wait to begin. Her story had not only pathos but depth. Ben was surprised to learn where they'd met and fallen in love—in a ski lodge—and married—in a little mountain chapel. Then followed the first wonderful years of their life together, perfect except, of course, for the lack of children.

Hedrick was busy taking notes. "And you've been married how long?"

"A little more than four years," Ben said, giving the information he and Kate had agreed on. He thought of reaching for her hand but decided this lawyer was bright enough to pick up on obvious phoniness. "Most of the adoption agencies won't consider a couple until they've been married five years or more, but we believe there are other more important considerations. Maturity, dedication—"

"And determination," Kate added. "We want a baby and we don't want to wait. That's why we're here. We want a baby now."

"For Christmas, Mrs. Black?" The lawyer's smile was sardonic, and it caused Ben to cringe, but Kate handled his remark perfectly.

"Well, of course not that soon. But maybe next year would be possible."

Hedrick nodded. "Possible."

He asked a few more general questions. Kate was eager to fill in with specific answers that ran just short of their life stories. Finally, Hedrick put down his pen.

"You're a charming couple," he said, "and seem genuine in your desire for a family. However, procedures must be followed. My secretary will give you an application to fill out, financial forms and a medical questionnaire for your doctors. There's also a small fee for processing."

"That's no problem for us," Ben said expansively, wondering what Hedrick considered small. "We'll cooperate in every way. I do have one question, though, something my wife and I have discussed. Where do these babies come from? What kind of mothers give them up?"

"First, let me say that all the children available to me for placement aren't babies," Hedrick responded, circumventing the question. "There is a great demand for newborns, so obviously the wait for them is longer."

"That doesn't matter," Kate broke in quickly. "A one-year-old ... maybe two..."

Hedrick nodded. "I'm glad you're flexible on the age because we often have parents who are forced to give up an older child for adoption. Whatever the preference, we do our best to make a good match with prospective parents. But all of those specifics will be addressed with great care once you enter the process."

"Can't you give us a general idea of where the babies come from?" Ben persisted. "Are your referrals from doctors, social agencies, word of mouth or—"

"We have various sources, all of which are private and confidential," Hedrick replied, his pale eyes unwavering.

"Then we'll never know anything about the child we adopt," Ben said.

"You might not know the birth mother's name, but information about the adoptive child will certainly be supplied. However, that's a long way off." He got to his feet. "And now if you'll step outside, Kim will get things started. Please take our packet of forms home with you and give serious thought to all of your answers. It's very important that we get correct information from the outset so that we don't encounter snags along the way."

Hedrick was polite but firm. Clearly, the interview was over. He shook hands with both of them and ushered them to the reception area.

Kim sat at her desk, the forms stacked neatly in front of her. She was dark, pretty and very thorough, taking her time as she explained each document that Kate and Ben were to return, her movements matching her Texas drawl.

When she finished, Kim commented, "I see couples all the time who want babies desperately, and I can tell right away how serious you all are."

"Oh, we are," Kate echoed.

"Believe me, I understand what you're going through," Kim assured her.

"I'm so glad," Kate responded. "We're just desperate for a baby."

Ben thought that was overblown, but Kim bought right into it. "I can tell you are, and I'll do everything I can to help. The reason I love my job so much is because I get to be there and see the new parents' faces on that wonderful day when we place their baby with them."

"I wonder if that day will ever come for us?" Kate asked dramatically.

Ben winced, and then thought what the hell? He might as well play the game, too, since Kim seemed genuinely interested in their case. She could have influence with her boss, even the answer to just how *much* money mattered.

"I told Hedrick that money is no object," he said. "Whatever it costs to get a baby, we'll pay. Even if it's not a baby. We like toddlers, too."

"It can be a boy or a girl," Kate said tearfully. Ben stopped her with a look.

"Don't you worry," Kim assured Kate. "You never know what can happen—a placement falling through, a desperate natural mother in need of help. Why don't you leave me your phone number?" she suggested.

Kate scrawled Ben's number on a pad. "Thank you so much," she said. "You surely are filled with the spirit of Christmas."

Ben choked back a laugh, covering it with a cough.

"You all might be surprised," Kim answered with a smile. "Sometimes things turn around real fast here."

"So WHAT DO YOU THINK?" Kate asked as they headed for Ben's car.

"I think you missed a career as an actress. Where did all those tears come from?"

"I'm not sure. Maybe it's the new hair." She patted her wig. "I wanted it to seem real."

"I think you succeeded," he said with a wry smile.

"Did I overdo it?" she asked. "I caught some of those killer looks of yours."

"I think Kim ate it up. As for Hedrick—" He shrugged. "I don't know how to evaluate him. He's bright and cagey, but is he a criminal? It doesn't add up," Ben decided.

"What were you hoping for?" Kate asked.

"Some hint of duplicity, I suppose. But he doesn't fit the profile of the person we're looking for. He's certainly not the type to leave a threatening message on your answering machine or go gunning for you in the streets, whatever the reason."

"There could be a whole ring of people working for him, Ben, just like Tina suggested. He may be the man at the top."

"If that's true, he picked a very dangerous criminal path. I can picture him more easily in high-stakes investments, money laundering, stuff like that. But kidnapping babies for adoption?" Ben shook his head. "I don't think so."

"What's the next step?"

"Wait a few days. If nothing happens, approach him again, and keep digging into his background. We can't rule him out yet. In fact, we can't rule *anybody* out.'' He opened the passenger door and helped Kate into the Bronco.

They were three blocks from Hedrick's office when Kate noticed Ben tensing over the wheel. He glanced into the rearview mirror, eyes narrowed.

"What?" she asked. "You look alarmed."

"Not alarmed," he said, smoothly changing lanes. "Curious. There's been a white pickup truck behind us since we left the lawyer's office. I know I'm getting overly suspicious, but—"

Kate started to turn and look over her shoulder.

"Use the side-view mirror," he warned. "Don't look back."

"Who could it be? I can't make out the driver," Kate fumed. "Can we make a run for it?"

"In this traffic? No, but I can try a few tricks. Are you game?"

Kate checked her seat belt. "Go for it."

"Keep your eyes open for the next parking garage, and get some money out of your wallet."

Kate fumbled with her handbag. "There's a garage up ahead."

Ben sped up and then without warning turned into the garage and grabbed a ticket from the automated machine. The pickup tried to turn, but overshot the entrance. The sound of honking car horns permeated the winter air as the driver attempted to back the truck and failed.

As soon as the automatic arm on the garage entrance lifted, Ben zoomed inside, circled around and headed out the exit on a parallel street. The parking attendant, taking the fees, looked surprised as Ben handed him a dollar for a minute's parking time and then roared out onto the street.

"You can look now," he told Kate. "Do you see a white truck?"

"I think we lost him."

"*If* he was following us," Ben said. "I may be seeing dragons where none exist."

"He did try to turn into the garage."

"So maybe he wanted to park. Still I think we'll take the scenic route back to Tina's, lots of cruising around so we can be certain no one is behind us."

"Why would Hedrick have us followed?" Kate asked. "Unless he somehow recognized me. *If* he shot at me— This gets more complicated by the minute. I feel so guilty involving Tina and you and taking up most of your time. Your business has probably gone to hell."

Ben laughed. "Your job at ESS was the last one I had scheduled for this year, remember? I'm heading for sunny Mexico soon, and I've got enough work in January to keep me busy."

Kate nodded and looked out the window. Even though it hurt, she needed to keep in mind that she and Amanda were only a temporary part of his life.

"Besides, this mystery you're involved in has become a full-time job for me. And you, too. As usual we have more questions than answers. Was the break-in at your office a coincidence?"

"I doubt it," Kate said darkly.

"And if not, is it connected to the person who may—or may not—have followed us?"

Kate sighed. "Despite what Tina says, this isn't like a TV movie. Nothing seems to make sense, and we certainly don't have all the loose ends tied together."

Ben chuckled. "Nope, we seem to be collecting more of them by the hour."

BACK AT TINA'S, they gave her an account of the interview and then discussed what to do about the ESS office. Tina was calmer, but not eager to return to work. Finally Ben made the decision. "I'll take Tina back to collect your messages, E-mail and one of your PC's. That way, Tina can access all the files, and we can switch the phones over."

"Great," Tina said. "Let's get the fax, too. Business has been slow, Kate, so I might as well work from here. With you out of the office, I'm not setting up interviews."

"Do it," Kate agreed. Somehow she'd square it later with the corporate office. Right now safety seemed more important than possible job placements.

After Ben and Tina left for the ESS office, Kate wondered how her assistant had handled Amanda. This was definitely not a baby-proofed place. Everything that was reachable was also breakable. And everything that couldn't be reached was what Amanda *really* wanted.

After a couple of temper tantrums, Amanda settled down with what Kate decided was an appropriate "toy" that couldn't be destroyed—at least not immediately—a colorful macramé purse that Tina had hung over the living room doorknob. As backups, she added a pan and a set of wooden spoons from the kitchen. That should keep the baby happy for a while.

With one watchful eye on Amanda, Kate picked up the phone. She was too jumpy just to sit. No matter what the Hedrick visit produced, she still had unfinished business of her own. Her first calls produced no satisfactory results.

Her inability to reach Robert Brownley at home or in his office was irritating. This time, the maid who answered the phone at his residence merely said he'd left for the day; the secretary at his office informed her that he was in off-site meetings. Was it possible that he'd been behind the break-in at her office? Deciding she needed to keep a low profile, Kate didn't leave her name and number this time.

She made the same decision when she called the spa and was told that Coral Lampiere was still on vacation, with her return date uncertain.

Kate settled back in her chair and thumbed through her address book for the other number she needed to call.

She immediately recognized the pleasant Southern drawl of her second cousin, Laura Knight. "Kate! We've been wondering about you. Haven't heard a thing since you got custody of the baby. How are the two of you getting along?"

Kate glanced at Amanda, who was busy chewing on Tina's purse.

"Right this minute, we're doing okay, but it's tough, Laura. I'm not the maternal type."

The responding laugh was low and supportive. "Don't be silly. All mothers feel that way. With my first, I was a basket case...."

Kate listened while Laura recounted her early days as a mother. Now in her late forties, she'd reared three children successfully, which, Kate figured, qualified her to give advice. She gave it generously.

"Jack and I learned by doing." She told a few anecdotes to prove that philosophy while Kate hung on, waiting for an opening. "You can learn the same way, Kate, just by doing whatever needs to be done—"

*But,* Kate thought, *you and Jack had each other.* She didn't say that though, since there was no reason to state the obvious. Instead, she equivocated until her cousin came up with an interesting suggestion.

"Why don't you and Amanda fly down and stay with us for the holidays? Florida has to be more appealing than Denver right now."

Kate laughed. "Well, it's certainly warmer, and that appeals to me," she admitted.

"Then come on down. Oh, maybe I'm intruding into your plans. Are your parents going to be in the States for the holidays?"

"No," Kate said quickly. "Not this year. So I'd love to join you and Jack." The invitation appealed to her, not only for the heat of the sun but for the warmth of a family. There was just one problem. During holidays, all Laura's immediate family gathered at the Florida house. "Do you have enough room for me and Amanda?"

"Sure. We'll make room. Our kids—though why I still call them kids when they're in their mid-twenties, I don't know—will be here, but we can double up. It'll be downright homey. Come on, say yes."

"Oh, Laura, you don't know how much I want to join you for the holidays. I really need help—you know, advice about Amanda, and from someone whose judgment I trust."

"Then it's settled." Laura sounded definite.

"Well, I don't know.... Reservations will be hard to get this time of year—"

"Call me if there's a problem, honey. Jack wasn't an airline exec all those years for nothing. He may have taken early retirement, but he still has pull."

Kate thought about Christmas. Ben would be in Mexico. She and Amanda would be—where? She wasn't even sure her own apartment would be safe to return to by then.

"Yes," she said decisively.

"All *right!*" Laura exclaimed. "I can't wait to see the baby. Who does she look like—Libby or Derek?"

"Hmm. A little of both, I guess. She has Libby's coloring but her—" Kate laughed. "I don't know, Laura. She looks like... a baby." Amanda crawled toward her and Kate scooped her up, cradling the phone under her ear and positioning the baby onto her shoulder. "I probably can't talk much longer. Amanda's on the move."

"I remember what that means," Laura said.

"But there's one other thing, Laura—" Amanda grabbed Kate's nose and then her cheek. Kate swiped at the baby's plump hand. "I was just wondering if there's anyone else in Derek's family we need to call. I know so little about him."

"I don't believe so, darling. The authorities asked me that before, and all I could remember was that his parents were both dead. Years ago, I think. I thought maybe there was a sister, but Jack reminded me that there was only the one brother...."

"A brother?" Kate asked. "What was his name?"

"Let's see... Harley, I think. Yes, that's it. Harley Baldwin. I don't think he and Derek were on very good terms." There was a long pause on the line. "Why do you want to know all this, Kate?"

"Because—well, because I feel such a responsibility about this child, and I want her to know her relatives." Kate felt guilty about the lie, but there was no reason to alarm Laura with facts.

"If the relatives are worth knowing," Laura added. "In the meantime, make your reservations, and call me back as soon as you can about the flight. Don't forget, you can stay as long as you want."

Kate hung up the phone. "It'll be fun to be with a family, Amanda. They're such nice people. God knows they were great parents for their kids and would be great parents for any kid." She sat back and gazed into Amanda's face, wondering if that realization had been the reason behind her call to Laura.

Kate hugged her tightly. "A fine mother I am, baby, one who doesn't know how to take care of you, doesn't know what you need or want. What's worse, I've put your life in danger." She looked down at the baby, focusing on her unbelievably clear blue eyes. "Or is it the other way around? Are you the cause of all this furor? I wish I knew the answer, Amanda."

## Chapter Eight

Two hours later, Ben, Kate and Amanda were back in the car. "The coast is clear," Ben said. "No one followed Tina and me to or from the office. Want to head home?"

"Not yet. I feel as though we ought to make use of the rest of the day while we're in Denver."

"Okay. We dealt with my favorite suspect, so what about yours? Brownley, I mean."

"Still can't reach him on the phone. Maybe we should stake out his office or his house. Wait for him to make a move."

"And waste a lot of time doing nothing."

"Okay, how about trying the spa again, seeing what I can find out about Paige Norcross—maybe her real name." Then she glanced into the back seat. "Cancel that. Amanda's had a long day, and I bet I'd get hung up at the spa again." She heaved a sigh. "I'm out of ideas—except..." She dug in her handbag for her address book. "We could check out Coral's condo. Since no one at the spa seems to have any information, maybe some of her neighbors will know where she is." She looked over at Ben. "You probably think I'm crazy, but I'm really worried about her."

"I don't think you're crazy, and I certainly don't want you to worry unnecessarily. You have enough problems without adding that woman to them. I guarantee, her cruise ship hasn't been lost at sea—"

"I don't think she's on a cruise," Kate said adamantly.

"Then let's find out." He started the engine and smiled reassuringly at her.

Kate was glad that the early-morning tension between them seemed to have eased. As long as they concentrated on taking care of business, everything was fine.

Ten minutes later, Ben swung through the main gate of Coral's complex, past a guardhouse without a guard. "Which building?" he asked, studying the gray clapboard structures. "They all look the same."

"D-9. It's over there."

Ben parked the van, but as Kate reached for the door handle, he stopped her. "You and Mandy wait here." He grinned at her as he stepped down from the van. "Didn't I tell you that I like to play detective?"

When he closed the door, Amanda woke up from her ride-induced nap and started to whimper.

"He'll be right back," Kate assured her, turning to retrieve the precious lamb that had fallen onto the car floor and put it in the baby's lap. But Amanda continued to pout as she watched Ben walk away.

Kate followed her gaze and saw him striding toward Coral's condo. *Striding* was a word she didn't often use, but it suited Ben perfectly. Oh, the fantasies she had about him. "Forget the dreamy stuff, Kate," she ordered.

"Da-da," Amanda called out.

"Don't even think it," Kate said. Then she sighed and added, "It was only a kiss. It's not going to lead to anything more. In fact, it probably won't ever happen again." But that thought didn't keep her from following the baby's gaze, looking at one of the sights she liked the best, the sight of Ben striding.

He was back quickly.

"Only one of Coral's neighbors was at home," he said as he climbed back into the van. "A Mrs. Andrews, a nice elderly woman. She knows Coral but only to say hello. Yes, she noticed that Coral hasn't been around lately. No, Coral didn't say where she was going or even mention a trip—"

"See? I knew it!"

"Hear me out, Kate. Mrs. Andrews said that wasn't unusual because Coral keeps to herself and wouldn't be inclined to tell the neighbors her plans. She doesn't have any pets to be watched and doesn't seem to have any friends among the condo residents. She leaves early, comes home late, doesn't mix with the others."

"Oh." Kate was deflated.

"But the mail has been picked up. There're no magazines or newspapers lying around. So apparently she told someone her plans and made arrangements ahead of time. Doesn't that make you feel better about your friend?"

"I suppose so, but I'd feel even better if we could find a way to get into her apartment—"

Ben started the engine. "No way, Kate. I'm not going to add breaking and entering to my list of sins."

"I guess you're right...."

"You *know* I'm right," Ben corrected, with a sideways glance that momentarily threw her off track and caused her to forget about Coral and everyone else in this strange mystery—except Ben, her guide through the maze.

She looked away quickly and got back to business. "I guess the next step is to pick up my car—which is ready at last."

Ben turned off the engine. "And then what?"

"Look for an apartment?" It was more a question than an answer.

"A drab, cold, furnished place for you and Mandy at Christmastime?"

"You make it sound so inviting," she said wryly, but he was echoing her own thoughts.

"Well?" he challenged.

"As long as we think someone is watching my apartment, I don't know what else—"

"You could come back to my place."

Just when she was trying to stick with business, he threw that at her! She didn't know how to handle it.

"What's the matter, Kate?"

"After last night, I thought—I mean—"

"Yeah, we were both a little awkward this morning because of that. I didn't mean to make you uncomfortable."

"You weren't the only one involved," she said. When he smiled, she looked away again quickly. "But we're both mature. . . ."

"Yes, we are," he said.

She wasn't able to read anything in that statement, if there *was* anything.

"We know nothing serious is going to develop between us." She paused, but he had no comment this time so she managed a little laugh. "Maybe it's just as well we got the kiss out of the way. Now we don't have to wonder—" She stopped and shut up. It was possible, if she kept babbling, she could talk herself and Amanda out of everything, including a place to stay. "I appreciate what you've done for Amanda and me," she said, taking a one-hundred-eighty-degree turn from the subject of their kiss.

He picked up on the serious vein. "We still have no idea who's after you. I wouldn't feel right cutting you loose or putting you up in a strange place." He turned on the engine again and this time pulled out of the parking slot. "I'm taking off for Mexico next week and there's no reason why you and Mandy can't stay at my place until I get back. You're safe there." He drove past the gate and onto the street.

Then she remembered her phone call. "We may not be here for the holidays either," she told him. "My cousin in Florida invited us to visit them for Christmas."

"That sounds like a good plan."

Kate tried not to wonder if she'd heard relief in his voice as she continued, "My cousin gave me another bit of information. Amanda has an uncle, her father's brother. I guess we ought to check him out, too, just in case."

"Will do," Ben said, "but if he wanted the baby, it seems likely he would have contacted you, rather than shooting first."

"Same goes for Daniel Hedrick," Kate commented.

"Which, in your mind, leaves Brownley."

She nodded. "Unless you have a better idea."

KATE WAS STILL thinking about Coral during dinner but had little chance to share her concerns with Ben. The Chinese food they'd picked up fascinated

Amanda, and she fidgeted and fussed to get both
hands into the Moo Shu Pork, and Beef and Broc-
coli. Finally, leaving Ben to clear the table, Kate took
Amanda upstairs for her bath.

With the baby settled in the tub, playing with her
rubber duck, Kate's thoughts again turned to Coral.
She was worried about her despite Ben's assurances
that Coral was simply on a well-deserved vacation. She
couldn't get her friend out of her mind, partly due to
their friendship, partly to their parallel lives.

It was true that her life mirrored Coral's. Coral lived
alone in a condo; she barely knew her neighbors.
Coral vacationed by herself and was totally involved
in her work at the exclusion of a personal life.

Wasn't that what her own life had been like? Until
Amanda. And Ben.

"Da-da," Amanda chortled, looking up with a
smile.

"Why do you do that at the exact moment I'm
thinking about him?" Kate asked the baby.

"No?"

"No!" Kate laughed. "You're some baby." She
squeezed the sponge over Amanda's round little body
and watched her giggle with glee as the water cas-
caded over her. Adding a little soap, Kate washed the
soft skin, in and out of the fat crevices while the baby
beat the water, splashing all over her bather.

"Enough! You're going to drown me," Kate said,
laughing as she picked up the wet squirming child,
wrapped her in a towel and held her close to her heart,
feeling a great surge of love sweep through her.
Amanda could make a huge difference in her life; she
already was making a difference.

But what could she do for the baby? What kind of life could she give her?

Amanda pulled and tugged Kate's ear with pudgy fingers and cuddled against her neck. Her warm squirming body felt so natural against Kate, who held her tightly, wishing she knew the answers to everything that was happening in her life.

She felt tears prickle her eyes and hastily wiped them away with her free hand. "Answers?" she murmured. "Right now I don't even know the questions. But I do know I love you, little girl, and I hope I can protect you and care for you." She kissed the baby's fat cheek, but Amanda's attention was already drawn elsewhere. Her eyes had fastened on the light fixture over the sink. She raised her hand and pointed.

"See the light?" Kate asked. "Light."

"Yight," Amanda repeated. "Yight!"

"That's it!" Kate said proudly. "Wait until I tell Ben what a smart girl you are." She smiled at the image of herself and the baby in the misty bathroom mirror. "That's how real families react, Amanda. Real mommies and daddies."

She tried to visualize a real family, not her own, certainly; maybe her cousins. "Jack and Laura," she told Amanda, "they're *real* parents." She stopped herself, steadfastly trying to push away the thought that popped into her head: maybe they would be a more suitable family for Amanda.

No! Families came in all sorts and sizes, and this was a family, too, she and Amanda. "For better or worse, babe," she said to the child's reflection, "mostly, on my part, for worse so far. But that'll change."

Amanda reached toward the two reflections in the foggy mirror and laughed.

OUT OF THE CORNER of his eye, Ben had watched Kate climb the stairs as he settled at the computer. Then he'd gotten back to work. Only his mind was still with her, going up those stairs, taking the baby into the bedroom. What next? Giving Amanda a bath, putting her on the bed with her lamb while Kate stripped off her clothes and changed into—what, a nightgown? He wondered if she'd bought one at the mall, but even if she had, it was wishful thinking to imagine he'd see her in it.

She would definitely keep on her clothes, and when she came downstairs after Amanda went to sleep, she'd be fully dressed, ready to discuss the next part of their plan. Of course, his agenda was the same. At least, that was what he told himself.

Just hours ago, he'd thought he was on to something. He'd been sure he'd be able to prove Hedrick was after Amanda. Then the police would take over, and Kate and Amanda would go back to their lives. But it hadn't happened. He still had no idea who had attacked Kate.

Besides, that wasn't what was on his mind, Ben realized.

He tried to concentrate on the screen, but he couldn't focus because he was listening to the sounds from the loft. Amanda laughing and giggling, Kate talking softly. Feminine sounds.

Family sounds.

What was it about those two that tugged at his heart? What was it about *Kate* that kept him from focusing on work? Usually, his relationships with women were uncomplicated affairs that lasted until he—or she—was ready to move on. If a woman was too demanding of his time, he gently extricated himself, and the woman understood—or said she did.

Kate wasn't demanding. She was incredibly independent and determined to take care of herself. But somehow she and the kid were occupying an extraordinarily large part of his life, which was all his doing. Because he liked more than the excitement of the mystery; he liked the excitement of *her*.

He went back in his memory to the day they met. Kate had been businesslike and harried. But that Kate was also the one who tried on the blond wig in the boutique, the sexy short-skirted, flirty, funny Kate. And then there was the Kate he'd held in his arms.

So many Kates.

He heard her footsteps on the stairs and called out. "I found out a little about Mandy's uncle, and it's not good."

"Uh-oh." She stood behind him. He could feel her warmth and smell her sweet clean scent.

He forced himself to keep his eyes on the screen. "Yeah, a bad-check artist with a few arrests here and there. Misdemeanors."

"Where is he now?"

"Don't know that yet, but I will soon."

Kate walked over to the fireplace, a look of concern on her face. "I don't like the sound of it. Petty criminal..." Her voice trailed off.

Ben turned off the computer and got up, stretching his arms above his head. "Don't worry. A guy like that wouldn't want a baby."

"Except maybe to kidnap and hold for ransom," she offered.

"Then why the attacks on you? With you out of the way, where would he get the money? It doesn't compute, Kate."

She sighed, dropped into a chair and leaned forward, trying to work the tension out of her neck. "Maybe *he's* into the baby-selling business, too, or maybe he works for some kind of syndicate. . . ." She shook her head. "These guessing games are fruitless."

"We're going to find the answer," he assured her.

She looked over at him, and he read the doubt in her eyes. With one stride he closed the space between them and put his hand on her shoulder. "Don't worry." He could tell she was trying to be optimistic, but her eyes gave her away. He rubbed her shoulder, pressing his thumb against her upper back. "Everything will be okay—unless you cop out on me—"

"Why would I—"

"Because your muscles have gone ballistic. Right now, they're in knots."

"I know. I'm pretty tense, and I ache all over from my workout at the spa. I could use a muscle relaxant."

"Forget the artificial stuff. Just leave it to me." He moved his hands again, placing them on either side of her neck. "Let your head hang forward." As she did, he added, "Relax."

Kate dropped her head, but how did he expect her to relax when he was so close and his hands were so warm and strong? As he moved his hands toward her hairline, he stopped, laughing.

"What's the matter?"

"It's that hair of yours again," he said, "getting in the way." He pushed the heavy strands aside. "Now I can get to your muscles."

Kate closed her eyes and gave herself up to his powerful, hypnotic touch as he worked the tenseness out of her aching muscles.

"Lean back," he instructed, and once again she did as he asked, tilting her head, feeling her hair flow down her back. As he stroked his fingers along her shoulders and neck, she felt a tremor run along her skin. A warm golden glow suffused her. Her breathing was rapid but no more so than his; she thought she could hear the dual beating of their hearts. "Is that better?" he asked, his voice a low whisper.

"Yes..." She leaned against him and was enveloped in his warmth.

A heavy silence invaded the room, broken only by their raspy breathing. Kate knew she should stand up, say good-night, go upstairs. But she didn't. Instead, she looked up at him. He'd taken the band off his hair and, like hers, it hung loose, dark and shiny. His eyes were black as coals, and she became lost in their depths.

She never should have looked up with the need in her face so apparent. It changed everything.

He dropped down beside her, putting them on the same level, their faces only inches apart. Then he leaned toward her and grazed her lips with his. The soft touch turned into a greedy kiss that went on and on until they both gasped for breath but still clung together.

"This is crazy," she managed.

"I know." It was, and he knew that he should apologize and give himself a chance to cool off. He couldn't do that with her in his arms or even in his sight. He'd have to go outside. Take a walk in the cold. Regain his sanity. But he didn't consider it.

Instead, he pulled her close and kissed her again, hungrily. He felt her tongue against his, explored the soft recesses of her mouth, ran his tongue along her lips. The heavy throbbing of his desire couldn't be ignored. He wanted her desperately, wanted to make love to her—here, now, in front of the fire, touching her, feeling her....

Ben felt her fingers threading through his hair, the softness of her lips, the hardness of her nipples pressed against him. His hands roamed her body until he discovered the bare skin beneath her shirt. When he heard her deep moan, his heart quickened.

She reached for him, pushed aside his flannel shirt and slid her fingers along his back with a touch that sent shivers throughout his body. "I want to make love to you, Kate," he murmured. "In front of the fire."

Her answer was to cling to him more tightly, and that was answer enough for Ben. He picked her up and carried her to the soft rug in front of the fire. He could feel its heat and see its warm golden glow. Or was it the heat from their bodies, the glow of their passion?

She hadn't released her hold on him, but now her hands trembled a little as she pulled his shirt from his shoulders and unbuttoned his jeans. His own hands were more demanding. He took off her warm-up jacket, tugged at the waistband of her pants and began to undress her. Then, to his surprise, his hands shook, too, making his movements awkward and clumsy. Even with that unexpected nervousness, he managed to remove the flimsy, lacy bra and panties. "Mall lingerie? You won't be needing them now," he whispered as he pulled off the rest of his clothes and lay down beside her.

Kate felt a sigh escape her lips. They were naked in the firelight that seemed to caress them softly, as they caressed each other. His golden skin radiated a bronze glow in the shimmering light, and his eyes flashed with desire. She lay back, opening herself to him and almost purring in delight at the pleasure in his eyes. He touched her breasts, ran his fingers over them, a soft feather-touch. Then he leaned down and kissed each one, caressed, rubbed his thumb across the hard nub of her nipples. Deep inside an ache of desire formed, grew, built.

"What can I do to make you happy?" he whispered. "I want to give you pleasure, Kate." His mouth on her breast was moist and hot.

Her words came out in little puffs of air. "Just... don't... stop."

He gave a low laugh. "I won't, not until we both have what we want."

As he continued to work wonders on her breasts with his lips, he explored the rest of her body with eager hands. Her heart pounded explosively with a wild frantic beat. Greedily, she guided him closer, closer, until they touched and she opened herself up to him completely.

She gazed up at his face, framed by the soft black veil of his hair, shadows from the firelight flickering across the hard planes and angles of his face. Their eyes locked, and he whispered, "This *is* crazy, Kate. And wonderful."

"Yes—" It was the last word she spoke. Then everything happened at once. She dug her fingers into the hard sinews of his back. He moved more fiercely, deeper and deeper inside her. She wrapped her legs around him, arching forward as waves of pleasure built and swelled and held them at the peak for an endless moment. Then his muscles stiffened, hers did the same; he gasped for breath, and so did she. At the moment when she felt she could bear no more, he exploded inside her, and she gave herself to him.

Sometime in the middle of the night they awoke and turned to each other again. Was it a dream then—or a fantasy come true? She didn't know and wondered if she ever would. She just gave herself up to whatever was happening....

Sleepily, dreamily, they made love as if in a kind of slow-motion film, shot in muted colors. The dwindling embers of the fire glowed warm and golden. All around them the light was soft blue. They threw back the covers, which seemed to billow in rosy hues. Through the window the night reached its darkest point and headed toward morning. Kate melded into Ben and let herself become part of him, and then she slept—and he slept—again.

THE NEXT TIME Kate opened her eyes, the dawn had begun to filter through the windows, and Ben was still sleeping beside her. She got up quietly and stumbled upstairs, into the bed with Amanda. Like Ben, the baby was asleep, but Kate, although drowsy, was awake, filled with wonder about what had happened between them—their first lovemaking, passionate and yet tender; their second, a dreamlike fantasy.

She felt vulnerable—and confused, wondering what Ben had taken away from their experience and what he'd be like in the morning. How would he act?

And more importantly, how would *she* handle the morning-after?

As it turned out, she didn't have to worry. With the morning came an easy rapport as he gave her a kiss, gave Amanda a hug and got on with breakfast. Just as before. Only different, Kate realized as her heart swelled with a love she knew she shouldn't be feeling. She fervently wished for the strength to fight it, to accept the night for what it was—a time of exploration and desire, a coming together of two people who, for a while, needed each other. Nothing more.

But because the night had given her so much, she wanted more.

Ben brought her a cup of coffee and touched her cheek lightly with his fingertips. "We had a wonderful night together, Kate. I'll never regret that it happened."

"I won't either," she said. And she wouldn't, but at the same time she was very aware of what his words really meant: *when this is over, then we'll be able to look back with fondness on a fabulous night.* That was all. Nothing more.

She forced a smile, and they continued with breakfast in a companionable silence. When the last of the coffee was poured and downed, Ben sat back, a satisfied expression on his face.

She tried not to let his physical presence overwhelm her as she asked, "What's on the agenda for today?"

She'd done it—she'd managed to form the question in a totally businesslike manner, even though all she could think of was him beside her, the nearness reminding her of last night, and the joy and pleasure she'd experienced. And then that slow-motion dream—or movie—or whatever it was... She tried to suppress a smile at the next thought. If Amanda weren't around, she'd probably be unbuttoning his shirt and pulling at his zipper right now!

Ben Blackeagle wasn't merely dangerous, he was dynamite. He was every woman's fantasy, and last night the fantasy had been hers.

She listened with one ear as he talked about Harley Baldwin and what he planned to do in order to track the man. He seemed energized and vibrant. That was what sex did for him, apparently, left him sure and confident. While she...

Kate could only wonder what in the world was happening to her.

When the phone rang, startling her out of her reverie and Ben out of his planning, he grabbed it immediately.

He listened carefully, and Kate could see the expression on his face change from casual interest to intense concentration. He motioned for her to bring him a pad and pencil, and he began to take notes. "Twelve noon at the Brown Palace. Okay."

He put down the phone and turned to Kate, his eyes snapping. "Hedrick's assistant called to set up a meeting. About placing a baby boy with us. Doesn't it seem strange that things are happening so fast?"

She sank down in a chair. Amanda crawled over and pulled herself to a wobbly stance, holding on to Kate's legs, fussing to get into her lap. Automatically, Kate picked her up. "What do you think this means?" she asked Ben.

"That Hedrick could be in the baby-selling business."

Kate held Amanda close. "Does it also mean that he gets babies however and whenever he can? Is Amanda one of the babies he'd like to get his hands on so he can sell her to a higher bidder? Would he kill me for her?''

"I don't know the answer, Kate. I wish I did."

"What are we going to do?" she asked.

"Meet 'em," Ben replied definitely. "And try to find the truth."

"Without calling the police?"

"I thought about that, but we don't have proof of anything. They only want to meet and talk about placing a baby with us."

"But at the hotel, not in his office. Isn't that strange?"

"Yes, I'll admit it is. Which is why we need to cover ourselves." He went to his desk, opened a drawer and rummaged around until he found what he wanted. "Mini tape recorder," he said, holding it up. "It'll fit easily into your handbag. We'll hear the story—and record it—then we'll decide what to do."

"But—"

"We need evidence, Kate. And facts."

He pulled her to her feet and enfolded her and Amanda in his arms. "This could be it, Kate, the end of the search." His hug was strong and full of enthusiasm.

"That would be great," she said, wondering if her words sounded as conflicted as she felt. Of course, it would be wonderful to live freely again. That was the up side. The downside was that she and Amanda would be out of Ben's life.

He gave her a quick kiss. "Let's get going. Call Tina and see if she can baby-sit again."

She nodded as she watched him take the stairs two at a time. Ben Blackeagle, on the warpath.

# Chapter Nine

The Brown Palace, like every other hotel in Denver, was overdressed for the holidays, with a huge Christmas tree in the middle of the world-famous lobby and swags of greenery everywhere. Ben gave the decor a cursory glance. He was only interested in meeting Kim and her boss. He crossed the rotunda with Kate by his side and headed for the Ship's Tavern. Kim was seated at a table near the front, but the guy with her wasn't Hedrick.

He took a second to register that fact and decide how to handle it. Then with his hand under Kate's elbow, he guided her toward the table. "We're missing Hedrick," he reminded her.

"I got that," she replied.

"Still play it as we planned, and be sure your handbag is on the table. But don't make it look obvious."

"Don't overdirect," Kate whispered. "I can handle my role. You take care of yours!"

Ben tried to hide a smile as they reached the table.

Kim introduced the sandy-haired man beside her as Rudy Hall. With his hair brushed back from a high forehead and his round, open face, he was the antithesis of Hedrick, more like an accountant or salesman than a high-powered legal mind. Who the hell was he? Ben wondered.

Without hesitation, Kim began her spiel, her eyes meeting Kate's and holding them compassionately.

"I've been thinking and thinking about you and how much you want a baby," she said.

"We're desperate," Kate replied, placing her handbag on the table.

Ben thought the gesture was a little less than subtle, but the waitress appeared just in time to negate any possible suspicions. Ben and Kate ordered coffee, while Rudy requested a beer, apparently not his first. There were three empty bottles lined up beside his place, which he didn't seem to want cleared away.

When the waitress was out of earshot, Kim continued. "I talked to Mr. Hedrick about your case, and he seemed to think—" She looked down. "I shouldn't be telling you this."

*But you will,* Ben thought, *or we wouldn't have been summoned here.*

Playing her part, Kate pleaded, "Tell us, please."

It took no more than a nanosecond for Kim to comply. "Well, the truth is, Mr. Hedrick said that you two would more than likely have to wait a long time for a baby."

"Oh *no!* How long?" Kate asked anxiously, into her role.

"Maybe four or five years—"

The gasp from Kate's lips sounded very natural, but with it her hand flew to her throat in a movement so sudden that she knocked the handbag off the table.

Ben cursed silently, hoping that it hadn't opened to reveal the tape recorder, or worse, that the recorder hadn't fallen out. He reached for the bag. So did

Rudy. Ben was faster. But when he picked it up, one end of the recorder was clearly visible. He covered it with his hand and pushed it back into the folds of the bag, not at all sure how to close the damned thing.

"I'm sorry," Kate said breathlessly, as she found the clasp and snapped it shut.

Good move, Ben thought.

The waitress returned with their beverages, and Ben watched Kate take advantage of the confusion to reposition her bag on the table.

An even better move, he decided.

"I *am* sorry," she repeated. "But just hearing that our wait would be so long—"

Kim was all concern. "I know, and I understand what you must feel. That's why I wondered—or Rudy and I did—"

"I'm her fiancé," Rudy inserted. "And we share everything. When Kim told me about your problem, I saw how affected she was. Of all the prospective parents she's seen go through Hedrick's office, she was most impressed by the two of you. I told her that we had to do something to help you folks. So..."

Ben sensed what was coming as Kim leaned toward them and lowered her voice. "Would you consider an alternate source?"

"Such as?" he asked.

"Maybe a mother who doesn't come directly through Mr. Hedrick's office. Maybe a woman who isn't equipped to take care of a child and who desperately needs money."

Ben equivocated. "I'm not sure..." It was a good idea, he thought, to show a little hesitancy, especially when he knew that Kate would be all enthusiasm.

And she was. "Of course, we're willing to consider any possibility."

"How much money are we talking about?" He continued the role of doubter.

"Well, I'd say around fifty thousand," Rudy answered.

Kate gasped.

Rudy seemed surprised. "Is that too much? Kim said you were willing to pay any price."

"We are," Ben said, "with reservations. For example, what guarantees do we have, and where does Hedrick fit into this scenario?"

Kim had the answer to that. "He's more a rules-and-regulations kind of person."

"Does he know about this meeting?" Ben asked.

Kim looked down without answering, but her companion had a response. "We have to go around Hedrick when we find couples who are special—"

"And have plenty of money?" Ben asked.

"Let's face it, yes," Rudy said.

"So I gather this isn't exactly legal," Ben suggested.

"Don't be so suspicious, Ben," Kate chastised. "They're trying to help us." Then she made a remark that Ben found fit perfectly into their plan. "My only concern is that there might be some danger involved. Could we be arrested for cooperating?" She inched her handbag toward the center of the table, and Ben smiled in satisfaction. She was a great partner!

"Let's just say we've done this before," Rudy responded, "successfully. So far no one has been disappointed. Kim works the inside," he explained, "and I work the outside." He couldn't seem to contain his pride as he added, "I have contacts who can help me find young expectant mothers who need money."

Ben grimaced inside as images of a baby farm played in his mind. "And I assume you've found the young woman who'll supply our child...." A woman who probably got only a small portion of the money, he thought.

Rudy nodded, and Ben fought back his anger and disgust.

"Actually, the baby hasn't been born yet, but as soon as that happens, he'll be yours. It's definitely a boy," he added proudly. "This is no scam, believe me. We're just trying to help."

"I'm sure you are," Ben agreed, repressing his feelings as he looked over at Kate. "So what do you think?" he asked, knowing her answer.

"I say yes. Yes, yes!"

"I sense some reserve on Mr. Black's part," Rudy said, his open face not so open anymore.

"Of course you do," Ben replied. "And for a good reason. We're talking an awful lot of money."

"Not for a precious baby," Kate argued, staying perfectly in character.

"What if we wanted to meet the mother?" Ben asked them.

Rudy and Kim exchanged looks. "That might be possible," she said, "but it would take time to arrange."

Kate clutched Ben's arm. "Please, darling, don't let's wait any longer. The baby's important, not the mother."

For a moment Ben appeared to think it over. Enough stalling, he decided. "All right. When do you want the money?"

"Oh, thank you, darling," Kate sighed, burying her face against his shoulder.

"The sooner, the better," Rudy said. "The baby's due any time now."

Ben decided to act quickly, get this over and done. "We'll have the payment tonight, but I'll want a contract with written guarantees about the baby."

"No problem," Rudy assured them. "None at all. Half the money down and half when you hold your baby in your arms." After a beat, he added, "Cash, of course."

Ben raised a dark eyebrow. "Of course. Oh, one more question before we go. Did you follow us after we left Hedrick's office yesterday?"

Rudy looked embarrassed. "Yeah, sorry. Kim gave me a call when you were in with her boss. She said you might be potential clients for us, so I thought I'd check you out, see where you live—"

"And see if we had the bucks to pay for a child?" Ben asked coldly.

Rudy shrugged. "A guy can't be too careful about who he deals with. But you fooled me, turning into that garage so suddenly."

Ben stood up and dropped a ten-dollar bill on the table. "Guys with bucks learn to be careful," he said. "Remember we don't like being followed or cheated."

Rudy's face paled at the implied threat. "No problem, Mr. Black. I'm on your side all the way."

They arranged a meeting time, and before Rudy could order another beer, left the hotel and headed toward the car.

"I can't believe it," Kate chortled. "It's Little Miss Helpful. It's Kim! She's running her own adoption racket in Hedrick's office, right under his nose. Do you think he really doesn't know about it?''

"Hard to say," Ben replied. "She could be his messenger. But I doubt it. They have to pay the mother and then split the rest." He shook his head. "Something tells me the profit wouldn't balance the risk for Hedrick. But we'll let the authorities figure that one out."

She handed over the tape recorder. "Did we get it?"

Ben pushed "rewind" and played a few seconds of the meeting. "Loud and clear. Good job. Now we go to the cops."

Kate settled herself in the car. "But does this baby-selling racket have anything to do with Amanda and me?"

Ben shook his head. "Damned if I know. I can see our friend Rudy slashing your tires, and I can even imagine him shooting at you with a rifle—but what would be the point?"

"If we followed Tina's scenario, Rudy would shoot me, and Kim could arrive on the scene with fake papers and spirit Amanda away in the confusion."

"But why?" Ben argued, "when they have their own baby farm?"

"That's a good question," Kate replied with a sigh. "Maybe the police can find the answers."

"WHICH ONES are they?" Kate whispered.

"Kim and Rudy aren't here yet," Ben said as he and Kate entered the Ship's Tavern restaurant.

"What about the plainclothes detectives from the police? The lieutenant we talked to said they'd be here somewhere." She glanced around the Ship's Tavern.

Ben put a calming hand on hers. "Don't be so obvious, Kate. I have no idea who they are, but I know they're here. Relax."

"Relax when I'm in disguise in the middle of a sting operation? Oh, sure." She studied the room under lowered lashes. Surely the elderly couple to their right weren't police officers. Nor the two well-groomed women in their thirties laughing over drinks at a table behind Ben. Maybe the solid-looking man with a crew cut to their left?

She was so intent on her speculation that she didn't see Rudy and Kim enter the room, and when Kim touched her shoulder, she jumped and gave a little yelp.

"Nerves on edge," Kate managed. "So excited about the baby...."

Rudy slid into a chair. "No need to be nervous, Mrs. Black. Everything is going to be great."

Kim smiled reassuringly. "We have the guarantee in writing that you wanted."

"I like to see it," Ben said.

"And I'd like to see the twenty-five grand," Rudy countered.

Ben reached under the table and pulled out a briefcase, which he deposited with a thump on the table. "Here it is, one half the payment in cash."

"You don't mind if I check?" Rudy asked.

"I'd be disappointed if you didn't," Ben replied.

Kate held her breath while Rudy popped the locks on the case but before he could open it, the two women at the next table moved in. The taller of them flipped open a badge and said, "Denver Police. Rudy Hall and Kim Minter, you are under arrest. Please put your hands on the table where—"

Kim was frozen in her seat, horrified, but Rudy, after a moment's hesitation, sprang to his feet, sending his chair crashing to the floor, and sprinted for the door. The smaller of the officers gave chase. It registered in Kate's mind that she was no more than five-two in her heels and fast as a gazelle. Rudy crashed into a waiter carrying a tray of glasses.

Rudy was spun around from the collision but almost reached the door when the police officer tackled him and knocked him to the floor.

Kate gave Ben a tremulous smile. "Never underestimate the power of a woman," she said.

IT WAS 3:00 a.m. when Ben pulled into the garage at his house. Strapped into her car seat in the back, Amanda was fast asleep. But she wasn't the only one. Slumped beside him, Kate was also sleeping soundly.

"Okay, ladies," he said, "we're home."

Kate awoke, groggy and disoriented. "So soon?"

"You've been asleep since we left Denver." He gave her a little nudge. "Here's the key. I'll get the baby. You go on in."

Kate stumbled through the door and got as far as the stairs where she plopped down, arms on her knees, head between her hands. She looked up when Ben came in. "I'm so disappointed."

"Yeah, I know. So am I."

"It's not over, is it?"

"For Kim and Rudy, it sure as hell is," he replied. "But not for us. They had nothing to do with the attacks on you. Airtight alibis for the time of the shooting."

She heaved a sigh. "So we helped solve a crime that has nothing to do with Amanda and me. One that in our great detecting we simply stumbled on."

"That's about it," he agreed.

"Well, it's left me exhausted." She looked over at Ben. "You don't look so great either. This has been a long night of waiting. All the statements to the police and the questions—" Kate struggled to her feet. "I want to sleep for days."

Ben made a move to hand over Amanda and then changed his mind. "You're too sleepy. I'll bring her up and get her changed. And by the way, you can't sleep for days, because we're back to square one. Tomorrow we start over trying to figure out who shot at you, pushed you and slashed your tires."

"Ohh," Kate moaned.

He took in her tired face. "Don't think about it now. Get some sleep, and I'll wake you around noon."

She mumbled her thanks and while he changed the sleepy baby, fell gratefully into bed.

KATE WOKE UP on her own, showered, dressed and was downstairs before noon—but not by much, and still feeling exhausted.

Ben had gotten Amanda up and was holding her in the crook of his arm while he punched computer keys with his free hand. He called out, "Coffee's in the kitchen."

Amanda squealed to be let down and crawled rapidly into the kitchen after Kate, who scooped her up. "You're fast enough for the Daytona 500, kid." She was trying to keep an upbeat mood even while feeling tired and discouraged. As for Amanda, the baby seemed to be on top of the world.

"If you only knew what was going on," she murmured, pouring juice into the baby's no-spill cup.

Ben appeared at the doorway, looking just as chipper as Amanda.

"Am I the only discouraged one in this group?" she asked.

"We've just been up longer," he reminded her. "But I do have some bad news."

"Oh, no." She sagged against the counter, coffee cup in her hand. "I can't take any more."

"Well, then let's call it good news. Harley Baldwin, Mandy's uncle, is not involved in your problems."

Kate busied herself blotting up the juice that Amanda had spilled from the no-spill cup. "How do you know that?"

"Because the guy's in jail. Has been for six months."

"Drat."

Ben raised an eyebrow at the unexpected exclamation.

"Now that Amanda can repeat almost anything," she whispered, "I'm cleaning up my language."

He nodded with a wry grin.

Kate followed him to the dining room table with her coffee—Amanda chugging along behind—and dropped into a chair. "You realize we've made no headway, Ben. None of our ideas so far has panned out. Yeah, we solved a crime, but one that had nothing to do with us!"

He didn't respond for a long time, and then he said, finally, "We have to face the facts, Kate. All this time we may have been trying to make connections that don't exist."

"Meaning..." She knew what he meant.

"Yes, meaning that what has happened to you, the attacks, may have had nothing to do with Amanda."

Kate picked up the baby and held her close, chubby damp cheeks against her face. "At least you're not a target," she murmured.

"But *you* are," Ben said. "And we still have to find out who's after you."

"So back to Brownley, Paige Norcross, the spa..."

"Yep. Which means back into your wig and tights."

"I guess you and Amanda will be hanging out at the Western bar while I'm at Sky-High."

"Been there, done that," he said with a grin. "No, Mandy and I are moving on."

He held out his arms, and the baby went to him as happily as ever. There was no competing with the attraction Ben had for Mandy, and something about that warmed Kate's heart. She'd never seen a man and a baby with such an affinity, and she didn't even mind being left out of their twosome.

"Who knows? We might go back to the mall and see Santa again."

"Better you than me," she responded as she headed upstairs to change. Each step beat a rhythm that reminded her that two female hearts had been captured by one wonderful man. But had they captured his heart, and if so, for how long?

EVERYTHING they'd done so far had been carefully planned, including the fake adoption meetings. As Kate got ready for her second trip to the spa, Ben had tried to give her a plan of action, but since they were starting at square one again it seemed impossible. There was no way to anticipate what she'd find there.

"Probably nothing," he'd said, but with a warning. "Be careful. Don't make any rash decisions. If something looks suspicious, just get out of there. Then we'll decide what to do next."

She'd tried to keep that advice in mind as she chatted with Edie, the plump woman she'd shared that exhausting step class with on her first visit. They sweated through the machines, and atop the treadmills Kate dropped questions instead of pounds.

But she didn't get many answers. Coral still wasn't around, and the tall, good-looking manager, Jennifer, who seemed to remember everyone's name, didn't remember Paige Norcross. Or so she said. It was hard to read her reaction. As for Edie, she was an open book, and she drew a blank on Paige.

"She's a beautiful brunette," Kate told her.

"They're all beautiful—brunettes or blondes. Look around you. Every one of them could be a model—" she grinned through the pain of the weight machine "—or a call girl at the very least."

Kate tried not to react as her new friend padded off toward the hot tub, but the suggestion stayed with her. Could it be possible... She shook her head as she checked out the spa, which was definitely populated by beautiful young women. Except for Edie, where were the clients who wanted to get in shape, lose weight, begin a nutrition regime? Everyone in this place looked like the "after" in a before-and-after ad. Then another beautiful image popped into her head. Paige Norcross. The best-looking one of the bunch, the woman who'd been with Brownley—and with how many others?

It was time to snoop! The first stop, she decided, would be Coral's office. She would never believe the spa was a front for prostitutes as long as Coral was running things, but Coral wasn't around. Maybe her disappearance had something to do with ...

With what? *Don't be absurd, Kate.* In all likelihood, she told herself, she was once again on a wild-goose chase, going off on a tangent because of a remark about prostitutes. Just the same, she would check out Coral's office.

She had a vague idea where it was, but she'd have to get there carefully, in a roundabout and surreptitious way. So she began at the Sky-High restaurant, a chic room with a regular menu for outside customers, which included women and men, and a special nonfat spa menu for members. She ordered Herb Chicken with grilled vegetables, and eyeballed the room filled with middle-aged men and young, beautiful women. That contrast certainly did seem to fit Edie's comment about call girls.

To make matters more interesting, as Kate left, she passed a corner table where an argument had erupted between two familiar people—Mark, one of the managers, and the good-looking heartthrob, Dylan, who seemed to be getting a dressing-down from his boss. Dylan's face was reddened, his voice defensive, a sign that he was fighting back.

Whatever was going on between the two men, at least it meant they were occupied and not looking out for Coral's office. On the floor of the gym, Jennifer was also busy. Now was the time!

Kate passed the lounge and moved on to the next door, where a sedate brass marker declared Private. She paid no attention to it as she pushed through.

Then she immediately wondered what in the world she was doing. Ben was the sleuth. She didn't have a clue how to proceed. But he had given her a good bit of advice: move quickly, look around, check things out and then get the hell away from the danger area.

With that in mind, she headed down the hall, passed the offices of the comanagers, Jennifer and Mark Kersten. Then she stood before the closed door of the one she was looking for, that of Coral Lampiere, owner and president.

She looked both ways. The hall was empty. She reached for the doorknob of Coral's office, took a deep breath and turned the handle. The door swung open, and she stepped inside. Her body trembled, as much with excitement as fear. This was it. She touched the light switch, illuminating the office.

Coral's office. She felt a sudden awareness of her old friend, an intimacy and a closeness, as she moved toward the desk. She stopped for a moment as the feelings swept over her.

During that pause, something happened. She hadn't heard anything, no turn of the knob, no footsteps on the carpet. But somehow she knew someone else was in the room!

She stifled a scream as his hand clasped her shoulder. Turning, she faced the buff, bald-headed Mark Kersten.

"What are you doing here?" he demanded.

"I . . . well, I was looking for—"

"The lounge?" he asked sarcastically.

She shook her head.

"The gym, the restaurant, what?" His face was close to hers and he still held on to her shoulder.

She tried to find her voice. "I—"

"Didn't you see the sign?"

"Yes, but, I was looking for . . . Coral Lampiere."

"Coral's on vacation," he said. "And this area is off-limits." His hand grasped her until she cringed in pain. Then he released his hold and stepped back.

"Sorry, I didn't mean—"

He didn't need to keep his hold on her. All he needed was to stand there, arms crossed against his broad chest, muscles bulging in his powerful shoulders. That was enough for Kate.

Like a frightened child, she bolted and ran.

# Chapter Ten

Kate dashed out of the spa and stood blinking in the afternoon sun, looking for Ben. She wasn't desperate, she told herself; she just wanted him—here now!

She glanced quickly at her watch—nearly time for Ben to meet her. It would be just her luck that he and Amanda were having so much fun at the mall they decided to spend the day with Santa and the hordes of kids. She looked back toward the spa, half expecting to see Mark chasing her. All was quiet, serene and peaceful.

Then the big mahogany and brass doors opened, and she headed for the street, not looking back to find out who was behind her. She caught her breath, watched the traffic whizzing by and had almost gotten up the nerve to dash across the street when Ben pulled up at the curb.

"Where did you come from?" she asked, breathless, as she slid into the passenger seat.

"We were parked across the street, and we saw you come running out as if a guided missile was after you. What happened?"

Kate hesitated. She knew if she told Ben that she'd poked around in off-limits territory, he'd be justifiably angry at the chance she'd taken. On the other hand, weren't they partners in their amateur investigation?

"Kate—"

She decided on a near-truth. "I had a little run-in with Mark Kersten. In fact," she added quickly, "I seemed to be running into or up against the entire staff. Jennifer denied any knowledge of Paige Norcross, though she prides herself on remembering everyone's name. And Dylan—well, he had problems of his own."

"What kind of run-in?" He was back to Mark.

"Nothing, really. He's just...creepy." She couldn't help shuddering when she thought about all the massive strength in the man's upper body.

Ben didn't press further except to advise her. "I think you'd better stay out of that place." He pulled into the traffic. "Ready for some big news?"

"Only if it's good."

"That depends."

"Ben!"

"Okay, okay. While you were inside, Tina reached me on the car phone to say that Robert Brownley called ESS. He's in his office and wants you to get in touch."

"He's finally ready to talk!" Kate reached for the phone, but Ben stopped her. "Before you make the call, take a deep breath, stay cool and think clearly."

She took a deep breath and tried to do the rest.

"Ready?"

She nodded and he handed her the phone.

"Don't say anything foolish."

"I KNOW WHAT'S on your mind," Kate said as they finally settled down to lunch at a neighborhood diner. "You think I should have arranged to meet Brownley at his office."

"I asked you to be careful about what you agreed to, and under the circumstances, his office would have been the safest place. He wouldn't dare try anything with his staff around."

"But the museum is just as safe. There'll be people all over, visitors, staff, even guards. It's no different from your meeting at the Brown Palace. That could have been dangerous, too. Besides, you'll be there as backup. Isn't that what the police call it?"

"We're not the police. And what about Amanda?"

Amanda perched on Ben's lap, plunging her spoon in and out of a bowl of mashed potatoes and getting them as far as her face but not quite to her mouth. "Maybe Tina could watch her while we're at the museum?" Kate offered tentatively.

Ben sighed. "She's already running your office from her home."

"Which is what I should be doing," Kate added.

"Don't start feeling guilty. You took a couple of days off during a traditionally slow time. Then there was an attempted break-in. Considering the situation, you're both entitled to a break. But we certainly can't double Tina's workload by adding Amanda to it."

"I know," she admitted.

"Kate, is there any way I can talk you out of keeping this appointment?"

She shook her head adamantly. "Brownley knows that I know about Paige Norcross, and he's ready to talk about it. You should have heard his voice on the phone, so conciliatory, so...well, almost humble."

"Maybe he's a good actor."

Kate leaned forward and wiped Amanda's mouth. "Drink your milk, Amanda," she said absently. "We won't know until I meet him." She looked at Ben earnestly. "We've ruled out Amanda's arrival as the cause of these attacks on me, haven't we?"

When he didn't immediately respond, she continued, ticking off on her fingers, "Amanda's uncle is in jail. Hedrick seems to run a clean operation. Kim and her boyfriend may be crooks but they're not after me. We ruled that out, too."

She paused for him to nod affirmatively.

"So that leaves Brownley and the spa and Paige Norcross. Doesn't it make sense that a prostitution ring is being run out of the spa?"

"It's a viable possibility," he admitted. "But that doesn't diminish the danger—it increases it. If Brownley tried to get rid of you twice because you saw him with a hooker, what makes you think he's Mr. Nice Guy now?"

"Because of his voice—"

"Kate," he said, shaking his head.

"And because he agreed to meet where I wanted. He could have said in a park—or at a roadside café, but the museum..."

"You could be shot at in a museum just as easily as on the street."

She tried to dismiss that thought with reason. "Too many witnesses."

"There were witnesses on the street," he countered.

"But there was also a getaway car. Isn't that what you call it?" she asked.

Ben managed a smile. "After bank robberies, maybe. In your case the shooter was already in the car."

"Yes, and all he had to do was drive away. Not so easy in a museum. It's the perfect place for me to meet him, Ben. Maybe they have a kiddie museum for you and Amanda—"

"No way am I leaving you alone with Brownley," he countered.

She pushed her plate away and slumped back in the booth. "You didn't bargain for being a full-time bodyguard when you showed up to fix my computer system, did you, Ben?" She meant the words to be light, but a serious tone had slipped into her voice.

"Let's just say when I took on the job, I had no idea it would be so demanding, but it's too late to back out now," he added jokingly. "So I'll call my sister and see if she can take care of Amanda for a while. She has a houseful of kids of her own—one more shouldn't be a problem."

"I knew you'd come through!" Kate flashed him a dazzling smile, and he felt his heart tighten in his chest. Every minute he spent with her got him more and more involved in her life. What the hell was happening to him? Whatever it was, he wouldn't stop until it was over. After that... He shook the thought away and stood up abruptly, handing Amanda to Kate.

"You clean her up. I'll make the call."

BEN'S SISTER'S HOUSE was on a well-kept street in the Denver suburb of Lakewood. A huge wreath adorned the door, and outdoor lights—blazing colorfully even though it was still broad daylight—were wrapped around two small fir trees. A couple of black-and-white cats raced across the porch and disappeared over the fence into the backyard where Kate caught a glimpse of a child's swing set and a jungle gym. Inside, a dog barked at their approach.

This was a house that celebrated Christmas, children and pets.

There was only a trace of resemblance to Ben in the high cheekbones and dark eyes of the woman who greeted them at the door. Joan Talmadge was short and a little stout with auburn hair and a wide smile. She immediately held out her arms to Amanda.

"What a cute baby!" The Blackeagle magic worked again and Amanda went eagerly to Joan, regarding her curiously but not at all fearfully, even though a fuzzy brown puppy scrambled at her feet.

Joan gave the dog a loving push with her foot, settled the baby more comfortably in her arms and greeted Kate. "Hi, I'm Joan."

"And I'm Kate. Thanks so much for baby-sitting for us."

"I'm happy to do it." She cut her eyes at Ben. "It's not often that my big brother asks me to take care of a baby for him."

Kate could tell that Joan was bursting with questions. Her curious eyes darted from Kate's face to Ben's, looking for clues, too polite to ask. Instead she said, "How about some coffee?"

Ben shook his head. "We've got to get moving. Kate has a pressing engagement." He handed Joan the laden diaper bag. "This is packed with enough gear to last for a week."

Just then two small figures burst into the room, grabbed Ben's legs and tried to shin up them like climbing a tree. He picked up one child in each arm and whirled around. Wild laughter ensued, and Amanda, imitating, joined in as the dog barked frantically and jumped around Ben's legs.

"This is my number-one niece, Nikki, aged four."

"Four and a half, Uncle Ben," she insisted.

"Sorry, Nik. And this is Tyler, who is two. Is *that* right, Nikki?"

"Uh-huh." The little girl was now giving all of her attention to Amanda.

"Where's your older brother?" Ben asked Nikki.

"Playing computer games. Can I hold the baby?"

"Later," Joan promised, "after you help me get her out of this snowsuit."

Nikki almost jumped with joy at the opportunity.

A few minutes later, Ben and Kate slipped out of the house, and Amanda hardly noticed their departure. All her attention was on the two dark-haired children wooing her with their favorite toys, and the puppy, amazingly gentle as he nudged her with his damp nose.

Kate paused in the doorway, and Ben noticed the expression on her face. "What's wrong?"

"Nothing," she said. "But something's very right for Amanda. Just look at her. She's glowing, with a real family, a mother and kids...."

Firmly he took her arm. "You're too hard on yourself, Kate."

She followed him to the car. "Sometimes I think I'm not tough enough." The rest of her thoughts she left unsaid. If she were really tough, she'd know what to do about Amanda, what would be best for both of them.

THE DENVER ART MUSEUM wasn't as packed with visitors as Kate had expected; in fact, it was almost deserted when they arrived. Apparently Christmas and culture didn't go together, Kate thought as they picked up maps to the special traveling exhibit where she'd suggested meeting Brownley.

"American impressionism. How did you know about this?" he asked.

"I read about it in the newspaper a few weeks ago. It's here through January so I didn't rush out to see it since I thought I had plenty of time." She smiled ruefully. "Obviously I didn't imagine what would happen in the meanwhile." Kate chattered on, trying to cover her nervousness, but Ben didn't hide his concern. They hadn't gone but a few feet before he began making negative noises.

"I don't like this, Kate. Not enough people around."

"You're around," she said lightly. But her heart was pounding in spite of his presence. Maybe she *had* made a mistake setting this up with Brownley in the museum, but he hadn't wanted to meet in his office or home, and she certainly wouldn't have suggested her office. No matter where they met, she would still be on edge.

"There'll be a guard in the room," she said, reassuring herself as they got closer to the exhibition. "Maybe you should walk behind me so Brownley won't see us together."

Ben dropped back, his words unintelligible. Kate suspected half of them were curses. But she was right, and he knew it; Brownley wouldn't approach unless she was alone.

She walked into the first room of the exhibition with Ben close behind, but not too close. There was a bench in the middle of the room. She walked over to it and sat down.

Ben moved around the room, looking at the pictures but not seeing them. "Damn," he muttered under his breath. "How does this keep happening to me?" He glanced around. There were two other people wandering from painting to painting, talking in low voices, finally moving on to the next phase of the exhibit.

They were now alone, Kate on the bench, Ben walking the room, one eye on her. Where the hell was the guard?

Another couple passed through, quickly, disinterestedly, followed by a lone man. Ben's body tensed. He made a quarter turn toward the door, watching but with his eyes still ostensibly on the painting. Three of them, alone in a huge room filled with valuable artwork—and no guard.

But this wasn't their man. He could tell by the expression on Kate's face. Damn, he shouldn't have had to wait for her reaction; he should have asked for a description of Brownley. He could only hope his amateurishness didn't get them into trouble.

Then a group of a dozen or more people came into the room, all middle-aged, most carrying catalogs, not the guides given away at the entrance but expensive books. Obviously a serious group, following their professorial docent, who stopped in front of the first painting and began what turned out to be a lengthy explanation of its merits.

Ben couldn't decide whether their presence was a detriment to their cause or not. Surely, Brownley would be less likely to try anything with a crowd around; on the other hand, they could inadvertently create a diversion for him. Ben circled the room, casually glancing at the pictures, and made his way to the one across from where Kate was sitting. He positioned himself between her and the door and stepped back to look at the painting, a large landscape resplendent in pinks and greens.

As he studied it, a stocky, middle-aged man in an expensive suit approached. He stopped a few feet from Ben, whose instinct told him this was Brownley. But as he turned from the painting to look around the room, his eyes swept past Kate to the members of the tour group, clearly none of them the right age.

He looked back at Kate, frowned and checked his watch.

What the hell was going on? Ben figured it out just as Kate waved the man over. He hadn't recognized her in the blond wig. At least the disguise was successful.

Too bad that he couldn't keep the woman wearing it under control.

He watched carefully as Brownley walked toward Kate, his hand extended, perfectly civilized. She remained seated on the bench but reached up and shook hands before gesturing for him to join her. So far so good. Ben quickly crossed the room and took a position directly behind them so he could watch without being observed by Brownley.

To his surprise, Kate reached up to touch her hair and actually wiggled her fingers at him behind her back. The woman was incorrigible.

"IT'S THE WIG," Kate was saying. From the moment she saw him, she felt certain that Brownley was no

threat, and she was proud of the wave she'd given Ben
to let him know.

"Yes," Brownley said, almost wearily, "I was sure
I remembered you as a redhead." He sighed deeply. "I
might as well get right down to it, Ms. McNair. I'm in
a very difficult situation."

Kate bit her lip, determined to keep quiet and listen.

"The woman you saw me with that night in the
house...well, she wasn't my wife...which you know,
since you've now met Martha."

"Yes," Kate said, carefully adding, "your wife
seems like a fine woman."

"She is and I love her very much. That...incident
with the other woman—"

"Paige Norcross," Kate blurted out, no longer
careful.

"You know her?"

"I know of her. That is, I saw her one other time."

Brownley digested that information. "Well, I
haven't seen her again, and I never intend to. That
night was a middle-aged man's foolishness, a momentary indulgence. I wish it had never happened."

"And do you wish I'd never seen you, Mr. Brownley?" Kate challenged.

He smiled faintly. "Yes, I must admit, I do."

Kate felt a momentary pang of pity for him. "I've
been trying to reach you for a long time," she said.

"And I've been avoiding you, trying to decide what
to do."

"Did you consider getting rid of me?" she challenged.

His expression was incredulous. "Getting *rid* of
you? You mean firing you? Canceling the ESS con-

tract? No, I've wanted you to have the contract from the beginning, but after you saw me with... Paige Norcross, well, I thought a lucrative deal might make you look a little more positively toward me."

"That sounds like blackmail, Mr. Brownley."

"On the contrary, Ms. McNair, I was wondering if you might be the kind who holds men like *me* up for blackmail."

"That's not my style, I assure you," she said.

His mouth tightened. "If you told what you saw at my house that night—"

"Your career would be ruined...."

"Along with my marriage."

Kate glanced over her shoulder and saw that Ben was now seated on a bench at the opposite side of the room, his long legs stretched out, his attention on a painting. He knew she was safe. What he didn't know was that the man she'd been afraid of was even more afraid of her!

"I'm no danger to you, Mr. Brownley, but I expect Paige Norcross could be."

"You mean she might tell my wife?"

"I don't know," Kate said honestly. "I don't know anything about Paige. Do you?"

He shrugged. "I know nothing about the woman. I met her at a cocktail party. We struck up a conversation, and she gave me her number. I was a little surprised, frankly, but when Martha went out of town..." He looked away, embarrassed. "You know the rest of the story. But maybe I don't," he observed. "Is there something I should know about her?"

"I'm not sure," Kate replied. "Have you ever been to the restaurant at Sky-High Spa?"

"Coral Lampiere's place? No, I've never been there."

"But you know Coral?" she asked eagerly.

"I met her once or twice at fund-raisers. That's about it. Did Paige work at the spa?"

"I don't know...." Had she been wrong again? Maybe Paige was only a patron of the spa and Edie's comment about call girls an offhand remark. "I saw her there and thought... It doesn't matter." As usual with her theories, two and two weren't making four.

Brownley gave a relieved sigh. "I'm glad I finally faced you." He looked at her beseechingly. "Of course, you'll keep the contract with United Charities, but because it may be difficult for us to work together, I'll have one of my assistants handle your job search for us."

"You don't have to worry," Kate said. "If we run into each other at United Charities, it will be as if this never happened."

Brownley got to his feet and said sadly, "But *I'll* know and *you'll* know." He held out his hand. "Merry Christmas, Ms. McNair. We'll talk after the new year."

"Goodbye, Mr. Brownley."

Thoughtfully, she watched him walk away. Ben was beside her before Brownley was out of the room. "So?"

"He confessed—"

Ben looked skeptical.

"To being unfaithful to his wife. Nothing more."

"I figured as much. He couldn't be scamming you, could he?"

Kate shook her head. "He's afraid of me, Ben. That's why he was hiding out. Now that he realizes I'm no threat, he has to worry about telling his wife."

"Do you think he will?"

"I don't know, but I put a little scare in him with talk of Paige. That might just prompt him to tell Martha. I hope so. She seems like the type who can handle it."

"Meanwhile, back to Paige..."

"I hate to say this, but I could be wrong about the call girl angle, too. He didn't hook up with her through the spa." She sighed deeply. "We're back at square one again, Ben."

"Maybe not," he said. "Hey, would you like to have a look at the rest of the exhibit? It's pretty interesting."

She shook her head. "Another time, when I'm more in the mood for art and less in the mood for puzzles."

"We've had a long day, Kate. Enough of puzzles for a while."

"No, Ben, I have another thought. Listen to this."

With a sigh he dropped down beside her.

"I was thinking about that chart you made of the events in my life before the first accident."

"Yeah, the night appointments with Brownley and Coral, the arrival of Amanda—"

"Three events. We've eliminated Brownley or he's eliminated himself. Amanda's connections aren't connections at all. That leaves the spa."

He raised that dark eyebrow, waiting.

"Maybe I did see something that night. Something I didn't even know I saw."

"You saw a janitor."

"That's all I can remember." She looked at him with a sly smile. "Do you think I should be hypnotized so I can recall the rest?"

He grinned. "Why not? We've tried everything else. Unfortunately, I don't have the necessary powers." He cut his eyes at her. "And if I did, I might be tempted to use them for something else."

She felt herself blushing. "You wouldn't need to hypnotize me to..."

"To?" He nudged her insinuatingly.

"To—whatever you were thinking."

"It's what I've been thinking about most of the day, when we weren't racing around putting pieces of a puzzle together."

"I have an idea!" she said.

"Damn." He leaned forward, elbows on his knees and looked at the picture directly in front of them, trying to get his mind back on their search. He might as well admit it. Kate was obsessed at this moment with only one thing, and it wasn't him. "Okay," he said. "Tell me."

"It's about the spa."

"Of course. Because of your friend Coral."

"And Paige Norcross and the call girl ring."

"If there is one."

Kate didn't seem to be listening. "Coral and I talked on the phone, we met for lunch, we made an evening appointment. If she wrote any of that on her calendar and someone saw it—"

"Where are you going with this, Kate?"

"I'm not sure, but I know Coral wanted to replace some of her personnel. And I can't imagine that person—or people—would be happy about it. Mark Kersten, for example. He's a tough-looking guy, really scary. He could easily be the kind to run an illegal operation."

"Because of the way he looks." Ben's tone told her he wasn't buying that.

"Then there's Jennifer. All warm and friendly on the outside, but cold as ice inside."

"You can tell that from the way she looks, too?" Ben was trying to play devil's advocate, but Kate wasn't ready to give up her line of thought.

"And Dylan—if there's a call girl ring, he could easily be the front or shill or whatever they're called, the one who lures women into the spa—"

Ben laughed in spite of her dirty look. "And then turns them into ladies of the night?"

"It doesn't work that way, right?"

"Right."

She couldn't contain an irritated frown.

"But you may be on the right track," he admitted. "The spa could be a cover for something."

"And with Coral gone, they have free rein to do whatever they want. God, she'd die if she knew."

Ben's voice was ironic. "The way you almost did."

Kate didn't want to think about that. "Maybe someone at the spa thinks Coral told me about the call girl ring. That makes sense! Listen to this—Coral finds out someone's running an illicit business out of her spa, and she decides to replace the person—or people."

"Go on." He looked interested now.

"So she calls me to find a replacement before she axes the culprit or calls the police. Someone sees my name on her calendar—"

"And decides you know too much?"

"It's possible."

"Then why wouldn't the bad guy—or gal—try to get rid of Coral, too?"

A shiver ran down her spine. Her cheeks felt clammy. "Maybe someone did."

The room was eerily silent as Kate's words hung in the air. Then a voice boomed out.

"Time to leave, folks. We'll be closing in five minutes."

They turned to see a guard standing in the door.

"*Now* the guard arrives," Kate said.

Ben called out, "We'll be right there. Just give us another minute or two with this picture." He turned back to Kate. "It's not plausible."

"Why not? You were going right along with me for a minute there."

"Here's what stops me—that out of all the phone calls, appointments, meetings on her calendar, they pick your name and decide to get rid of you. Too convenient, Kate." He stood, gave her a hand and pulled her to her feet.

"Then . . . what?"

"There's still that night. You must have seen something, or someone thought you did."

They left the room and walked down the deserted corridor, their footsteps echoing on the marble floor.

"If only I could remember . . ."

"A janitor, that's all?"

"Hmm," she murmured.

"What was he doing?"

"I tried to ask him a question, but he was busy cleaning up. . . ."

"With a broom, with a vacuum cleaner—with what?" Ben prodded.

"No, he was pushing a trash thing. He just kept going."

"Trash *thing?*" Ben chuckled.

"You know, those big canvas things they dump all the wastepaper baskets into."

"Was anyone with him, helping him?"

"Nope. Damn. Why aren't I more observant?"

"Don't worry about it. Whether you saw anything or not, I'm beginning to believe that they think you did."

"Suddenly you see the light!"

They left the building into a late afternoon that was crisp but not as cold as it had been. Kate didn't even bother to zip her jacket as they headed toward the car. "What convinced you?" she asked.

He laughed. "Your persistence. No, it's the idea that Coral..."

"Found out?"

He nodded.

"Ben, we have to do something! Coral could be in danger—or worse." She grabbed his arm. "If there's an illegal business being run out of the spa, there'll be records. Probably buried in a computer file. Someone like you could find them." She looked up at him pleadingly as he opened the car door for her.

But she had to wait for his response until he got in, started the car and drove away. Even then he was silent for a long while.

"Ben..."

"There's a limit to what I can hack into, Kate. If I could get in through a modem, maybe, but the spa's personal computer system...I doubt it."

She paused a beat before offering her next suggestion. "What if you were inside the spa—after hours?

Then you'd have plenty of time to hack around, and while you were doing that, I could go through Coral's desk and look for the name of her travel agent, her cruise ship—''

"No, Kate."

"What choice do we have?"

"I told you before, I draw the line when it comes to breaking in."

"We wouldn't have to break in. We could just hang around until the spa closes. If we accidentally get locked in, it's not our fault, is it?"

"We're picking up Amanda and going home." Ben pulled onto the turnpike and headed toward Lakewood.

"Then I'll go alone," Kate said with stubborn determination. "If you aren't interested in getting to the bottom of this, I can't force you to help. God knows, you've done more than your share."

"And willingly, Kate," he reminded her. "But I stop short of going to jail."

"We won't get caught, Ben, and if we do, we just say that we were . . . uh . . ."

"Making love in the linen closet and time got away from us?"

She was determined not to smile. "*I'm* going, unless you tie me up or handcuff me—"

"Now *that* sounds like fun."

She ignored him and continued. "We say that we didn't realize the spa closed so early, and we were just about to call the police to extricate us. No one can call us on that."

"Except someone with half a brain."

"I'm going anyway."

"How're you getting there, Kate?"

"In a cab, if I must."

He shook his head. "Not a good plan."

"In my car. It's certainly ready now."

"You mean the car that had its tires slashed, the one that's about as recognizable to the wrong person as your red coat?"

"I'll get there—somehow. And I'll get into Coral's office. Either you're with me or not."

"Not."

But Kate caught something in his voice. She could tell he was weakening; she knew deep down he was intrigued. She had learned to read his thoughts, which both encouraged and saddened her. It showed how close they had become but reminded her that the closeness was only temporary.

Quickly, she got back to her argument. "It'll be a challenge...."

He didn't respond.

"A wonderful hunt."

Silence.

"You know you're dying to do it and just too stubborn to give in. Admit it. You want to know the answer as much as I."

"I'll only admit that I'm not letting you go alone. If you're right about the spa and Coral and the call girl ring, this could be dangerous."

"Not if we're careful. My disguise has worked perfectly at the spa. No one knows I'm Kate McNair, Coral's friend from ESS, and besides, they'd never try anything there. You should see the place. It's crowded with women on the machines, taking classes, in the Jacuzzi. And the restaurant's always packed." She decided not to mention her lone foray into Coral's office where she had been accosted by Mark.

Ben pulled the car to a stop two houses away from Joan's. They could see her and the children in the yard, building a snowman. At least the older kids were building. Amanda was grabbing hunks of snow from the round body as fast as the others added it. Soon a snow fight ensued, with the kids tumbling about, laughing and squealing while Amanda clapped her hands in approval.

For a moment, Kate forgot her argument with Ben. "Look at Amanda," she said, "holding her own with the others and loving it."

"Mandy adapts fast," Ben said.

Kate nodded, unable to stop watching or thinking about how happy the child was, how right it was for her to be with a family. The messages seemed to be coming louder and clearer all the time: Amanda would be better off almost anywhere than with her.

"Let's pick her up," Ben urged.

"No. Let her be happy for a few more hours. She needs a break from me."

"Don't be down on yourself, Kate. You're getting there."

"I'm trying."

Ben took in the scene once more. "But I see your point. She's having a good time, and the kids are crazy about her. So..." He turned the car around.

They were on the turnpike before Kate's mind left Amanda and got back to their plan—or lack of one. "Ben..."

He glanced over at her.

"Since we have time to kill, why not take a run by the spa, just to check it out?"

He heaved a sigh. "I might as well agree because if I don't, you'll never give up, but we have to do it my way, Kate."

She smiled innocently. "Of course, Ben. I wouldn't think of doing it any *other* way."

# Chapter Eleven

Parked near the back of the spa, Ben watched delivery trucks come and go. There seemed to be no end to deliveries to Sky-High Spa, even as darkness fell. Two women in running suits with Green Thumb logos on their jackets carried in a potted palm. Aren't We Clean? made deliveries of laundered towels, and a skinny redheaded kid hefted a carton of Fruity-Tooty drinks and disappeared through the delivery entrance.

But the white truck from Poolside People interested Ben the most. It had been parked at the curb since he pulled up. As he watched, a hefty young man came out of the spa carrying pool-cleaning equipment, which he loaded into the truck. He wasn't wearing a uniform; there were no logos on his shirt.

"All *right,*" Ben said aloud. This would be his way in.

He waited patiently as the pool truck drove off and then forced himself to wait another fifteen minutes before making a move. He'd promised Kate that he could get into the spa and hide out until closing time. That was the trade-off to keep her from finding a way to let him in. He was worried enough about her getting past the receptionist and into the locker room without being noticed by Mark. Ben sensed, whether she admitted it or not, that something had happened during her last visit, and he didn't want to take any chances this time.

He checked his watch. Time to go.

He walked to the delivery dock and rang the bell. Nothing happened. "Damn." Was he too late? He waited and then rang again.

Finally the door opened and a harried young woman in a warm-up suit greeted him. "Another delivery?" She saw that he was empty-handed. "What now?"

Ben smiled to himself. She was overworked, and he couldn't have been happier. "I'm from Poolside People."

She looked confused. "Your guy was already here."

"I know. But we forgot one important water test." He shook his head. "This is embarrassing to admit, but..." He took a chance. "The guy we sent is new, and he made a mistake. We wouldn't be the city's leading pool cleaner if we didn't make sure everything was perfect."

He looked down at her with a sly smile. "We aim to please." He stuffed his hand into his pocket. "It's just a simple test. Only takes one dipstick."

She shrugged. "If Coral were here, I'm sure she'd want everything to be perfect, but she's gone and Jennifer's busy—"

"And you're overworked," he said sympathetically.

"You're right about that." She sighed heavily. "It's too late for repairs, deliveries or anything else, but go on in."

He paused. "Sorry, but I've never been here so you'll need to point me in the right direction."

BEN LISTENED to the closing sounds inside Sky-High Spa. Doors shutting, lockers clanging, voices calling out goodbyes. Stretching his legs, he shifted slightly in the tiny changing stall. How normal-size people managed to get out of their clothes and into bathing suits in these places, he didn't know, but it could be worse, he decided as he settled down to wait.

A few minutes later, he heard the sound of the door to the pool area opening and held his breath. A man's voice called out, "Anybody in here? It's closing time. This is the last call." Apparently satisfied that the area was empty, the staff member flipped off the lights and closed the door.

Ben looked at the face of his watch, the only illumination in the tight space. Ten after nine. How much longer would he have to wait until he could safely unfold his cramped body and get out? Impatient, he decided on ten minutes; then, wanting to be cautious, he changed that to twenty minutes.

To pass the time, he turned his thoughts to Kate's most recent theory—that the spa was a front for an elaborate call girl ring. It sounded like a good theory, Ben admitted to himself, but Kate had absolutely no proof. Was her idea another dead end like all the others? he wondered.

In the darkness, Ben shook his head and smiled wryly. Who would have thought, when he arrived at Executive Search Services to handle a simple security job, he'd end up playing James Bond? No, not just Bond! Was there a spy character who also doubled as a daddy? Probably not, but it might make a great sitcom, Ben decided. Only what they were about to do tonight wasn't all that funny.

Especially Kate's role. She'd have to get past the reception desk and the exercise room without being spotted by Mark or Jennifer. Even though Ben hadn't heard the full story of what happened on her last junket into the spa, he knew that if any of her theories were right, Mark would be on the lookout for her, and his questions would be his wife's questions, too.

Ben took a deep breath, uncurled his body and opened the changing-room door. Dark. Quiet. Both good signs. He'd calculated the distance from dressing room to pool door, and in the dark he easily skirted the pool, pushed through the door and headed for the exercise room, using Kate's directions as a guide to the executive offices.

She was there to meet him.

"What kept you?"

He couldn't help smiling. The woman was remarkable. "Oh, a little thing called caution."

"Never heard of it." She laughed, but he could tell from the way she sounded that she was scared to death. He kept that observation to himself.

"Where'd you hide?" she asked.

"Pool changing room, just as you suggested. How about you?"

"Shower stall. It was clammy but fragrant. Everything around here smells great."

"I noticed that," he said, inhaling a scent that had nothing to do with the spa but was Kate's alone. He tried to ignore it and concentrate on what they were here for. "Now, let's get going—"

"Did you have any problems?" she asked.

"Not a one..."

"I didn't either," she told him. "Slipped right past the receptionist, never saw Mark...."

"Kate, we'll talk about our espionage experiences later. Right now, let's get organized. I don't want to spend more than an hour here."

"Will that give us enough time—"

"See to it," he ordered. "You take Coral's office, and I'll check out Mark's and Jennifer's."

"They left on the hall lights," she said. "Pretty convenient."

"These buildings never sleep, which is a good reason to get a move on," he nudged. "Let's get going."

KATE OPENED the door to Coral's office and closed it quickly behind her, before turning on the light as Ben had instructed. Then she flew to the desk, grabbed the December calendar and flipped through it. She was looking for two dates—her lunch appointment with Coral and the night meeting that never happened.

All the appointments were written in pen, she noticed as she went through each date. Good. They'd be difficult to doctor so if... She stopped, flipped back and then forward again. Her heart skipped a beat. Both pages pertaining to her had been torn out!

Had Coral ripped out the pages—or had someone else gotten to the book, the same someone who attacked Kate and who might have harmed Coral? Ignoring for a moment Ben's instructions to hurry, Kate sank into the desk chair and took a deep breath. There was no disputing the facts, but missing pages in a diary would mean nothing to the police. She had to find something else.

She opened Coral's desk and began methodically to rummage through it. No travel folders. No cruise brochures. Not a single notation that Coral planned a trip.

The door opened, and she jumped, startled.

"Don't go creeping around like that," she admonished.

"I thought that was the idea," Ben teased. "Quiet, creeping searches. Find anything?"

"Pages are missing from her calendar."

"Your pages?"

"Yep."

"What else?" he asked.

"It's not what's here but what isn't—no hint of a cruise."

Kate got up so he could sit down at the desk and turn on the computer. "That stuff could be at her house."

"I doubt it. Now I'm sure she's not on a cruise. That's just what they *want* everyone to think. Did you find out anything in their offices?"

"Nothing incriminating. Jennifer's a fitness freak with a drawer full of granola bars and low-fat cookies. As far as paperwork is concerned, she seems to run the day-to-day operation, instructor schedules, workout programs, that sort of thing. Nothing financial."

"And Mark—"

"Girlie magazines everywhere."

"I knew it!"

Ben didn't seem to be listening as he hit a series of keys on Coral's computer.

"He's running the call girl ring," she insisted.

He shook his head. "The spreadsheets look legit in the ratio of income to expenses. The spa does a good business."

"No wonder. He probably makes most of the money on the side with his sleazy operation," Kate said, not giving up.

"Umm. The figures aren't *that* good, Kate. Profits are in the normal range. Nothing extraordinary."

"Then it's hidden away somewhere," she insisted, "buried in a innocent-looking file."

"Don't think so. I'm pretty good at unearthing hidden files." He continued to hit computer keys, pausing between each series. "Damn."

"What's the matter?"

"None of the obvious codes work." He paused to think for a moment before shaking his head. "No, that's too simple."

"What?"

"Her name. What did you say it was before she came here?"

"Carol Lam—"

He'd hit five keys before the last name was out of Kate's mouth. "I don't believe it. She used Carol for her password." Ben shook his head. "Three easy accesses in a row. This place should have hired me to hack-proof."

Kate laughed. "Especially since you always leave a back door open."

"Only until I'm sure my clients know what they're doing."

"And I don't?"

"Nope." He looked up at her with a wink. "Maybe I'll give you a few lessons once all this is behind us."

She cocked her head and frowned slightly. That was the first time he'd mentioned anything that hinted at the future, even if it was only business. She started to respond, but he was back to the keyboard.

"Let's see what we have here..."

The moment was gone, and it was clear that he hadn't even noticed it. He was teasing, and she was taking it seriously. She bent over, trying to concentrate on the screen.

"Hmm, this is interesting. Look at the file named Xmaslist."

"Christmas cards, I imagine," she said as he opened the file. "My name's probably in there."

Ben chuckled. "Oh, I don't think so. Not in this one, anyway, unless your name is Scarlett or Bambi...or Paige."

"Oh, my God, it's the hooker list!"

"Looks like it. Beside each name is a number—" He hit a few more keys. "Some kind of code. Okay, I've got it. Separate subfiles on each woman, more codes, more numbers..." He turned to Kate. "Be patient. This may take a minute."

She glanced at her watch. "Besides the janitor, do you suppose there's a night watchman?"

"Probably. We'll just have to hope his rounds aren't hourly."

"Or even every two hours," she said. "It's past ten...." She stopped, afraid of putting pressure on him.

But he wasn't listening. His concentration was total, and Kate had no choice but to wait, standing by nervously until at last he uttered what sounded like a victory cry.

She focused on the screen as he told her, "It's all here. Dates. Times. Escorts, as they're called. And— fees. Look at this, Kate, they charge astronomical rates. This isn't some streetwalker fifty-dollars-an-hour deal. We're talking top-of-the-line prostitutes.

Three, four, five *grand*. And your friend Carol, alias
Coral, is the brains behind the operation.''

"No!" Kate protested. "It can't be true. It's not
possible. Coral is so... nice."

"The two things aren't mutually exclusive. Haven't
you heard about the madam with the heart of gold?"
He exited the document and hit the print key. "This is
quite an operation, Kate, bringing in huge amounts of
money. It's mind-boggling."

He leaned back in the chair, stretching, almost lan-
guidly, as the desktop printer began spitting out pages
while Kate, dumbstruck, slumped in a corner chair.

It wasn't possible that her mentor, her teacher, was
involved in something so sleazy. She remembered the
last time she'd seen her friend, now known as Coral,
at lunch in a downtown restaurant. Her hair, worn
short, was tinted a becoming shade of blonde, and her
neat trim figure was shown off to advantage in a de-
signer pantsuit. She looked much younger than her
forty-plus years. She was warm, witty, charming. How
was it possible, Kate wondered, that such a together,
classy-looking woman was running a call girl ring?

"Ready?" Ben asked. "Let's hit the road."

When she didn't respond, he got up and touched her
shoulder. "Kate?"

"It can't be true," she said in a muted voice. "I was
sure Mark was the ringleader. How could Coral have
done something like this?"

"One word," Ben said coolly. "Greed with a capi-
tal G. Obviously, your friend Coral has a secret side."
He ripped the list from the printer and tucked it into
his pocket. "Now *I'm* beginning to agree with you
about her vacation. I think it could be bogus."

"Should we call the police from here?" Kate asked, getting to her feet.

"Sure. We'll tell them we broke into the spa and gathered all this information by hacking Coral's computer. I don't think so, Kate. Getting arrested for burglary won't do either of our careers any good."

"What happens next?" she asked in frustration.

Ben took her face in his hands. "Let's talk about that after we get out of here. We've done all right so far. Don't worry." He kissed her quickly. "That's for luck."

"I needed it," she said, holding on to his strength for a moment. "Okay, I'm ready. Let's go."

She led him down the hall, through the reception room to the spa entrance. As she headed for the door, he grabbed her arm and pulled her back.

"What's the matter?" she asked, frightened.

"Nothing—yet. But this is the only area with outside windows. It's too exposed. Plus there's an alarm," he added, pointing to a yellow box at the entrance. "Better go out the delivery door."

"Won't there be an alarm there, too?"

"Probably, but it's closer to the car and not so exposed. Come on." He grabbed her hand and headed for the door he'd come in almost two hours before.

"Yep. There's the yellow box."

"We can't get out," she said in near desperation.

"Oh, we can get out all right, and the door'll lock automatically behind us. But the alarm will definitely sound."

"Can't you bypass it or something?"

"I know computers, Kate. I'm not a master electrician."

"But there's a number pad so there must be a code...."

"Sure, but security companies are a little more careful with their codes than the managers here at the spa. I might be able to crack it if we had all night."

"But we don't," she said, looking nervously at her watch. "Wait, I have an idea. What if I call the security company, tell them I'm Jennifer and I forgot the code—"

"Yeah, and they'll take your word for it. No way, Kate." He looked her up and down. "How're your legs?"

"My *legs?*"

"Are you all toned up from the machines?"

"Well, my thighs could be better, but I'm getting there. A few more sessions on the leg press and—" She stopped mid-sentence. "This isn't the time for teasing, Ben. We could be in trouble."

"You're right, and that's why I asked about the legs, because they're going to have to get you to the car in Olympic-record time." He moved to the door. "When I open this, I want you to run like hell. My car is parked about a hundred yards from here, at the end of the alley—"

"Why so far away?"

"So nobody would connect it with this place."

That made sense. But a hundred yards...at top speed ... Kate wished she had more spa workout time under her belt.

"The car's locked so stand by the passenger door—"

"Yeah, like I'll get there first." Her heart pumped with alarming speed as the enormity of what they'd done finally hit her.

"The alarm's going to be real loud. Don't let it frighten you," he advised.

"Oh, no. Of course not," she replied sarcastically. "Ben, I'm already as frightened as I'm going to be."

"I doubt it," he said under his breath.

"What?"

"Nothing. Just that the alarm will alert the night watchman. We'll just have to hope he's not nearby."

"And if he is?"

"Run even faster," he suggested.

She began to tremble. There was a very good chance they'd get caught. And arrested. And booked. Reporters would come. Newspapers would carry the story. Maybe eventually they'd prove their case, but it wouldn't matter because by then her job would be history.

She'd be in jail, and Amanda would be in limbo.

"That kiss you gave me for luck . . ."

He looked down at her, his eyebrow cocked.

"It didn't last long enough. I need a little more encouragement."

With a smile he leaned over and kissed her again, this time more thoroughly. "How's that?"

"I'm ready to try out my legs."

Ben turned the handle, the door opened and they rushed into the night.

FOR A FEW SECONDS all was quiet except for the noise of their feet pounding across concrete.

Then the sound of the alarm cut through the night with an endless wail. Kate raced beside Ben for a few seconds, until, just as she expected, he outdistanced her. That was okay. He'd get to the car, start the engine, and then she'd be there.

She felt a sharp catch in her side and slowed down for an instant. Her breath came in short gasps, and her heart pounded with the turbulence of a bass drum. Damn, she cursed to herself, she was in no shape to run a hundred-yard dash. About halfway to the van, clutching her side, she tried to speed up.

That was when she heard the footsteps behind her and a voice yelling out for her to stop.

The night watchman!

Kate wasn't about to stop, even though she was nearly doubled over from the pain in her side, and her breath was coming out in short, sobbing gasps. She was determined to make it, especially when she heard the sound of a car door opening and slamming, the engine starting. Ben was in the Bronco!

But the guard was closing in. She could hear his breathing, almost as ragged as her own. She was almost there. Just a few more steps—

A hand grabbed her jacket, pulled hard and stopped her in her tracks. She tried to lunge forward, but he held fast.

"No, you don't—" His voice was raspy and deep, and somehow Kate knew that the man was as winded as she. If she could only break away. She whirled, lashing out with her fists. "Let me go," she cried.

Then Ben was there. She heard a dull thud, the guard dropped to the concrete and she was free.

Ben dragged her toward his car, holding her arm tightly. "Get in." The driver's side door was open, and he lifted her high enough to propel her inside, across the driver's seat. She scrambled out of his way as he vaulted in and slammed the door.

As they sped off, she looked out the back window to see the guard lying in a crumpled heap. "Is he—"

"He's all right. Just knocked the wind out of him long enough, I hope, to keep him from getting the license number."

He stepped on the gas and propelled the Bronco around a corner just as Kate saw the guard struggling to his feet. "I don't think he had time to see the number," she said. "Unless he saw it before you hit him."

"No way. He was too busy trying to capture you." Ben made a sharp left, then a right. The alarm was still wailing as they came to an intersection and he pulled out into the traffic. Only then did Ben hit the headlights and slow down.

Kate let out a shaky breath. "We're okay, Ben. We made it!" Adrenaline pumped through her body, energizing her. "Oh, boy, what a trip!"

Ben threw back his head and laughed. "You're a hell of a date, Kate McNair."

BEN PUSHED the car to the maximum speed. Even if the watchman hadn't seen the tags, even if there were no police cars in sight, there was an urgency inside him to get home. Fast.

And her name was Kate.

He'd called his sister in advance and asked if Amanda could spend the night. In case of repercussions from the break-in, Joan's house would be a safe haven. To be honest, Amanda's well-being was only part of the reason for his call; Kate was the rest. He wanted her alone for a night.

She'd taken off the blond wig, and her hair fell damply around her face. She looked incredibly provocative as she pushed her hair away with nervous hands and looked out the window, seeming to watch the night fly by.

Was she as keyed up as he? As anxious? As much on fire?

It was difficult to tell when they were both silent...expectant, as if there was an unspoken agreement about what would happen when they got to his house. He stepped on the gas and the Bronco leaped forward, its headlights eating up the dark mountain road.

The excitement of their adventure, the thrill, still hung thickly in the air; it enveloped them both, and heated the already charged atmosphere.

Seated beside Ben, Kate clasped and unclasped her hands. She was possessed by an overpowering urge to reach out and touch him. She closed her eyes and tried to control her raging heart, but it was impossible. Her whole body vibrated with need for him. What was happening to her? She'd never had this kind of hot yearning before, never wanted a man as she wanted Ben. Now. This minute.

She took a deep breath and let it out through open lips. *Calm down,* she cautioned herself. *We'll be home soon.*

But her body still throbbed with memories of his kiss and touch, their lovemaking, the feeling of him inside her. She wondered if her legs would be strong enough to climb the stairs from the garage to his house. From his living room to his bed.

It didn't matter. If she couldn't walk, he'd have to carry her. That would be just fine.

ONE SMALL LIGHT burned when they finally reached Ben's living room. "Do you want me to build a fire?" His lips were close to her ear, his breath sending shivers along her spine.

"No," she whispered, admitting, "I have enough heat for both of us."

She met his eyes boldly, and he saw the fire there. His arms enclosed her and he pulled her toward the stairs. At the bottom of the stairs he stopped, unable to go another step, and pressed his body hard against her. The clothes she wore felt heavy, keeping him from her.

"Let's get rid of these...." His hands shook as he peeled off her jacket, shirt and bra, leaving her naked from the waist up. He let his hands roam her skin, stopping to place one over the curve of her left breast.

"Your heart," he said. "It's pounding so..."

"The chase. The excitement."

"Right," he agreed wryly. "Me, too." He kissed her hard, and while his tongue and lips explored hers hungrily, she pulled at his shirt, opening it to his waist. Then, struggling with his zipper, she pushed it down and reached inside to touch him.

He felt as though rockets had gone off inside his head. Swaying, he grabbed on to the railing. "I don't think I can make it upstairs."

Her laugh was soft and low. "Don't worry. We can make love here."

"On the stairs?" he asked as he buried his face in her hair.

"Have you ever..."

"No. Have you...?"

She shook her head as she sank back slowly.

He held on and dropped to the stairs on top of her. "I wonder if this is possible..."

Her throat was so tight she could hardly speak. "With us anything is possible."

He knelt in front of her and hungrily kissed her mouth. Warm liquid heat flowed through her as if she'd been freed from a winter's chill. He broke the kiss, and their eyes met and held. His handsome bronzed face was intense with pleasure. She leaned forward and kissed him, mating her tongue with his, pressing her damp skin against him. Just as their bodies touched physically, she yearned to be part of his heart, part of his life—forever.

And then there was nothing but the moment and the magic of being together.

WHEN BEN OPENED his eyes, it took him a moment to realize where he was, what had happened to him, whom he was with. But when it came back to him, it came back with a wash of emotion.

Kate was curled up next to him in his bed, a strand of her red hair splashed across his shoulder. He stayed quiet, barely breathing, feeling her close and reveling in the feeling.

He shifted slightly, and she eased away from his body for a moment. He felt alone and empty, and then she murmured and rolled back closer, cuddling against him. That was more like it. He smiled and ran his hand along the softness of her back.

What a time they'd had.

Both of them, high on adrenaline from the chase at the spa, had used their energy in a way that had resulted in a night he'd never forget. First their love-making on the stairs, which had been spontaneous and highly passionate. Later they'd showered together and made a meal of sorts before stumbling to bed. He'd expected that they would fall asleep then, but to his amazement, he found that he wanted her again...and that she was just as eager for him.

He opened his eyes and twisted a strand of her bright hair in his fingers, whispering, "You're quite a woman, Kate McNair. You're getting under my skin...which isn't what I had in mind. But..."

He thought about getting out of bed and going downstairs to make coffee, but Kate was still nestled tightly against him, and the bed was still warm and inviting. There would be a tough day ahead of them. Why rush it?

# Chapter Twelve

"What a great night that was," Ben said, squeezing Kate's hand as they walked along a winding path in the woods behind his house.

"It was a pretty wonderful morning, too," she responded and then felt her cheeks redden.

He looked down at her with a grin. "Is that a blush I see?"

"No," she denied.

"Well, you sure weren't blushing last night—or this morning," he added.

She remembered vividly their wonderful lovemaking, and then she really *did* blush.

His eyes held her, and his smile caused her to smile in return. "Were you?" he prodded.

"It was dark!"

He laughed and gave her a hug. "We'll have to remember to turn on the lights."

She nodded without reply as they walked on. He hadn't said "tonight" or even "next time." She listened to the silence of the outdoors, broken only by the sound of their feet crunching on the icy edges of the snow. She had no idea whether there'd be a tonight or a next time.

He helped her up a rise where they sat on a huge rock with indentations that perfectly accommodated their bodies.

"I carved this for us," he said.

"*Sure* you did." She settled comfortably onto the rock and heaved a sigh. Before them rose the jagged snow-covered peaks of the Continental Divide, etched against the wide blue sky.

"Beautiful, isn't it?" he asked.

"It's overpowering," she said, barely able to take in the whole panorama without turning her head, first to the left and then the right. There was so *much* sky, she thought. "I guess this is what they mean by 'big sky country.'"

"Yup," he said with a Western twang. "This is it, ma'am."

"It's fabulous."

Ben put his arm around her shoulder and gave her a hug. "Not as fabulous as being curled up in bed with you."

She didn't blush this time but looked him directly in the eye. "No, not as good..."

"But?" he nudged.

"But we have work to do, and we couldn't have done it in bed."

"We could have tried."

"Ben—"

"All right. We needed a walk in the crisp mountain air to clear our heads and subdue our hormones." He kissed her behind her ear. "Temporarily."

She leaned back beside him, letting the sun warm her skin and seep through into the depths of her body. "The sun on my skin..." she said, tilting her face upward and closing her eyes, "feels so good."

"That's what's so surprising about Colorado weather. We get these warm days in the middle of winter, but then we get a foot of snow," he added.

"That won't happen in Mexico at Christmastime," she said, feeling a momentary pang of jealousy. "The weather should be perfect down there."

"Umm," he replied idly, letting his fingers play in her hair. "No surprises south of the border. It's a different world. But the sun will be shining in Florida, too," he reminded her—and himself—thinking of what was ahead for both of them.

Instead of anticipation at his upcoming vacation, he felt a sudden wave of sadness. He shook it away, determined to keep his priorities straight. First, solve Kate's problems; then, take off for Mexico.

"But before either of us goes anywhere," he said, "let's figure out what's happening at the spa."

"Face some facts, you mean. Like the fact that Coral was running a call girl ring..."

"That's looking more and more likely."

"And someone found out and decided to make trouble."

He nodded.

"And she called me to find a replacement," she continued, ticking off the facts as she saw them, "and—he killed her."

"By 'he' do you mean Mark Kersten?"

"Who else?"

Ben shrugged, looking up into the clear blue sky. Above them a hawk made giant, lazy circles over the pines. For a moment, he thought about his grandfather, the times they'd spent together in the forest, and wondered if the old man could have put all these clues together any better than he.

"So, why wouldn't Mark turn her over to the police instead of killing her?" he asked.

"Because he wanted in on the deal?" she suggested.

"Sounds reasonable. But we can't take that to the police."

"Unless he killed her," Kate suggested.

Overhead, the hawk continued to circle. "There's no evidence, Kate," he reminded her. "No body."

She shrugged her shoulders in a frustrated gesture. "I know, and everyone at the spa seems to believe she's on a cruise."

The sun reflected on the rocks and on the bright snow, sending shards of light upward toward the soaring hawk. It was a beautiful scene, Kate thought as she leaned against Ben, feeling the warmth of his body merge with the sun's heat. But the beauty around her couldn't blot out the jumble in her mind or the half-formed ideas and images. Coral as she'd last seen her. Mark's anger. Jennifer's cold eyes.

"One of the people at the spa knows where Coral is." She spoke the thought aloud.

"And that person thinks you know something or saw something that puts your life in danger."

That thought still frightened her, in spite of the comfort of Ben's arm around her and the security of his nearness. "I didn't see anything that night but the janitor—"

"And he saw you."

"Definitely."

"Were you wearing your red coat?"

She nodded.

"Without a hat—your red hair hanging down for him to see?"

"Yes, but I don't think the janitor is a likely suspect."

"Unless he wasn't a janitor. Think about it, Kate. You pretended to be a blonde. I pretended to be a pool guy. Couldn't someone just as easily pretend to be a janitor pushing a cart that's big enough for—"

Kate grasped his arm with a moan. "Big enough for a body!"

"That could explain a lot. A missing body. Someone on your trail. What else can you remember about the guy?" he prodded.

She closed her eyes and tried to dredge up the memory. "A little above medium height, between five-ten and six foot, I'd say."

"Mark's height?"

She nodded. "But Jennifer's, too. And Dylan's," she added.

"Anything about the clothes?"

"Nope. Dark. Nondescript," she replied.

"You couldn't see the face?"

She shook her head.

"Hair. Didn't you say Mark was bald?"

"Yes. And both Jennifer and Dylan have blond hair..."

"Which was it? Think, Kate."

"I'm thinking so hard it's giving me a headache," she shot back. Eyes still closed, she worked on the memory. "Wait! I didn't see any hair—because the janitor had on a hat, no, a cap, a knit cap."

"That could have hidden long hair...."

"Or a bald head," she added, sinking back against him. "Masquerading as a janitor is a perfect disguise. Just think about it. The janitor could have been Dylan or Mark or even Jennifer. Taking Coral's body from the building in that cart and hurrying off when I asked about the spa hours. We need to find out who it was."

"First of all," he admonished her, "the body in the cart is just another theory, and if you remember, our detecting is definitely nonprofessional. I was totally wrong about Hedrick and Mandy—"

"And I was off base about Brownley."

"But you scored on the call girl ring."

"After Edie at the spa put the idea into my head, and then I was sure Mark was running it—but maybe I'm finally right this time. Practice makes perfect." She got up and began to pace in the crunchy snow.

"The janitor practically *ran* from me. I should have realized at the time how weird that was. Why would he run unless he had something to hide? If there was just some way to confront the staff at the spa...."

"Kate, I doubt if any of them is going to confess."

"Not willingly, but if there was a way to—"

"No more breaking and entering," he cautioned, letting her pace, but bracing himself against whatever scheme was brewing.

"I have a great idea," she said, her eyes bright with excitement, "one that's safe and simple."

"No, Kate."

"Listen, Ben. It's as simple as—" she looked down at the footprints she'd left in the snow "—as tracking with your grandfather when you were a kid."

Ben laughed. "The animals we tracked didn't have guns."

"But they were dangerous unless you knew how to outsmart them." She stopped in front of him, blocking the sun. "We can outsmart Coral's murderer by drawing him out, tricking him into meeting me."

"I'm not using you as bait. We tried that with Brownley."

"And it worked," she reminded him.

"Because he was a frightened man, not a murderer."

"Aha!" she said. "So you admit one of them is a murderer."

"I'm not admitting anything, Kate." He couldn't help laughing. "And we're not opposing lawyers arguing in court."

"No," she agreed. "We're detectives working on the same team." She leaned over, put her hands on his shoulders and kissed him. "And this time, we could be on the right trail for a change."

"MARK KERSTEN, please." Kate gestured for Ben to pick up the other phone. "He's coming," she mouthed.

"Kersten here."

Kate tried to speak slowly and calmly, but her first words were rushed. "This is Kate McNair. I need to meet with you."

There was a pause and then, "Do I know you, Ms. McNair?"

"In a way. And I know you...at least, I know something about you—and Coral, and what happened to her."

His voice was brusque. "Hey, what the hell is this? You sound like some kind of nut. I'm not listening to—"

Quickly, Kate jumped into her prepared speech. "Meet me at five o'clock this afternoon at the Cherry Creek Mall. I'll be sitting on a bench by the fountain.

By the way, I have red hair, and I'll be wearing a bright red coat. You remember that, don't you?''

"Lady, I got no idea what the hell you're talking about."

"You're a smart man, Mr. Kersten, you can figure it out. When you do, I'm sure you'll decide to be there."

She hung up the phone and looked at Ben. "So, what do you think?"

"Either he has nerves of steel or he knows nothing."

"When I said my name, he hesitated before he answered. That could mean—"

"A lot of things. I don't think he'll show, Kate."

"Well, I do, but just in case, I'm going to call Jennifer."

"Why bother? He'll tell her himself—"

"Not if he's in this alone," Kate said. She frowned, deep in thought. "Or *she* could be in it without *him*. Anyway, I'm calling her. Then Dylan. It's possible that—" She decided to keep her last bit of speculation to herself.

"Suppose they all show up?"

"They won't. Only the guilty party will be there," she said with determination.

"And you. And me, sticking by you like glue."

"No, Ben. The shooter knows what you look like. And a six-foot-two, hundred-and-seventy-five-pound bodyguard isn't that easy to camouflage."

"That's what you think."

"A disguise?" she asked with a look of disbelief.

"Wait until you hear my ho-ho-ho's."

KATE HAD TROUBLE convincing herself that they were, as Ben had warned her on the way to the mall, on a deadly mission. How could anything be serious, much less dangerous, in the crush of all these Christmas shoppers? Over the sound of recorded carols, babies howled, mothers called to children running off in all directions, wives scolded husbands laden with packages, and Santas pretended to be jovial.

Among them, Ben Blackeagle. With his cheeks rouged to a rosy glow, and his muscular torso well-padded, he made an impressive-looking Kris Kringle, she had to admit, but he wasn't playing the merry part of Santa well at all. At nearly five o'clock, she'd taken her place on the bench with Ben hovering nearby, looking grim and not at all Christmassy.

"You're too close," she said out of the corner of her mouth. "Move away and do something jolly."

"Ho-ho-ho," he responded, unconvincingly. "I'm just as Santa-like as the dozen other bearded men in red suits around here. The place is crawling with them. Must be collecting for some kind of charity."

She started to answer just as a little boy approached Ben with a determined look. She suppressed a grin and tried to overhear the conversation.

"Are you a real Santa?" the boy asked.

"Of course. That is, I'm a real Santa's helper. You may have noticed lots of us around."

Kate smiled to herself at that sensible explanation. She'd always wondered how parents explained all the different sizes and shapes of Santas around the holidays.

"Where's the real one?" the boy asked.

"At the North Pole, of course, getting ready for Christmas."

"Then if you're a Santa's helper, let me sit on your lap." His round eyes were hopeful.

"Well, I can't do that because..." Ben hesitated. "I'm the *standing* Santa. I bet there's a sitting Santa around here somewhere."

The child didn't seem convinced, but his response was drowned out in the din of Christmas music. From somewhere, a band had materialized, brass instruments blaring.

As Ben tried to detach himself from the persistent child, Kate glanced at her watch. Ten after five, and not a face from the spa anywhere in sight. Ben was probably right. This was a dumb idea. The call seemed to have baffled Jennifer as much as Mark. As for Dylan—he'd assumed Kate was a woman who wanted to meet him for a date!

She decided to give it until five-thirty. That would probably be about all the Santa-ing Ben was up to. Besides, even though Joan had been generous about keeping Amanda, they'd imposed on her long enough.

She turned her head to look toward Ben and the little boy, when she saw a red suit looming beside her. "Ben, how did you—" She looked up and realized this Santa wasn't her Santa at all. He was shorter, and his face was almost obscured by the big white beard.

When he spoke, his voice was low and gravelly. "I have a gun in my pocket, and I won't hesitate to use it. Stand up now and walk beside me."

Somehow she found her voice. "You wouldn't shoot me, not here in front of all these people."

"The hell I wouldn't. I'd kill you and probably hit a couple of kids, too. Now move."

She did as she was told, but not before one frantic look in Ben's direction. He was leaning over, talking

to the little boy, only a few yards away. So near, and
yet so far! She felt the gun being jammed into her side
and started walking.

Ben, tired of the little boy, had made eye contact
with the kid's mother and given him a little shove in
her direction, ignoring the complaints.

"Mom, this Santa won't let me sit in his lap."

"Sorry," Ben said. "Not in my job description." He
turned back toward Kate, only to find that she had
walked away through the crowd with another Santa,
and she hadn't looked back. What the hell? He knew
she would never leave without him. Unless—

Ben began to run, pushing aside everyone in his
path, wondering how she'd gotten so far away, so
quickly. "Stop that Santa!" he called out. "He's kidnapping the woman in the red coat."

People turned to look at him, surprise—even fear—
on their faces. As he forced his way through the
crowd, he heard the mumbled comments.

"Crazy..."

"Dangerous..."

"Call security..."

But Ben kept on running and kept on yelling.

And Kate heard him. His voice echoed across the
mall and into her brain. It filled her, gave her hope—
and made her fight. She stopped, digging her heels
into the floor of the mall, pulling and pushing, struggling to get free. Then she felt the cold metal of his gun
against her skin and stopped her struggle.

He pushed her violently, into a wall, through a door,
down a stairway. This was no spontaneous reaction.
The man knew what he was doing and where he was
going. Kate and Ben had made no such plan. But Ben
was a tracker—he wouldn't let her get away!

If she could delay long enough for Ben to see which way they were going, Kate was sure he'd find them. In spite of her fear, she struggled harder. But she was no match for this Santa.

Desperate, she tried going limp and slumping against the wall. He was there to grab her and push her forward, not caring if she missed a step, moving faster than she could imagine—down a flight of stairs, onto the parking deck.

He flung open the door and they crashed through— right into a pair of middle-aged women just getting out of a car. The force of their forward motion almost knocked down the women. As Kate was thrown into the taller, more solid one, she yelled, "Help! Get help!" Then she screamed in pain as her captor twisted her arm sharply back.

"Call security," he ordered. "This woman is shoplifting. I'm an undercover officer taking her in."

As they rushed away, Kate could see the women had their doubts. They stood for a moment, like statues, indecision on their faces, and then they scuttled like rabbits, heading for the stairs.

Kate looked after them, hoping they would be her saviors. Then she and her captor reached a car, and he threw her against it.

She hit the fender so hard the breath was knocked out of her. Still, she struggled, aware that she was going to have to fight her hardest now. If she was forced into the car and out of the mall, that would be the end. She would be as good as dead.

She kicked with all her might, out in front and then behind. She missed, missed again, and then hit her mark with her booted foot. She felt a thrill of pleasure when the Santa let out a moan of agony.

Then the agony was all hers.

Something hard and cold hit her head and sent waves of intense pain radiating through her body.

BEN THREW OPEN the door into the stairway and stopped short. Had Kate gone up or down? A misjudgment on his part could cost her life.

In that instant, a security guard barreled in behind him, shouting, "Hey, mister, stop right there."

A weathered-looking cowboy type, old but lean and probably in good shape—that registered first. Then he saw the glint of metal in the guard's hand. He wasn't prepared for armed security, but if he stopped to explain, he'd take up precious time. And Kate's life was in danger!

Ben turned and with a sharp upward thrust knocked away the gun. Startled, the man hesitated. With all the strength he possessed, Ben charged forward, hit the guard low and hard and pushed him back against the wall, where he slumped and then slid to the floor.

Ben made an instinctive decision and bolted down the stairs. He didn't stop to think or pick up the gun; he didn't stop for anything until he reached the bottom level and threw open the doors.

"Oh, no!" a woman wailed. "Another Santa! We just saw someone being arrested—by a Santa," she added breathlessly.

"Where?" Ben shouted, tearing off his beard and hat and throwing them aside.

The women shrank against the wall but one of them pointed, "That way."

Ben surged ahead as the woman muttered to her friend, "And you said shopping would be relaxing!"

He saw a car backing out, driven by a bearded Santa. Without hesitating, he raced toward it. His breath came in gasps as he pounded down the concrete. He had to get to Kate.

She prayed Ben was coming for her, but she had no way of knowing from her position on the floor of the car. There was something warm and sticky in her hair, and she felt as though a herd of elephants was racing through her head. But she was alive—and she knew Ben was out there. That gave her hope and enough strength to force herself to a sitting position. Spots of light flickered in her eyes, and the pain was almost overpowering, but she was spurred on by a familiar sound—Ben's voice, calling out her name.

The car stopped, shuddered and shot forward again, and with every ounce of strength she possessed, Kate pushed herself up from the floor. Weak and groggy, she fell forward against the Santa at the steering wheel and tore at his beard, ripping it off to reveal his handsome baby face and his long blond-streaked hair.

Ben reached the car as it surged forward, and he wrenched open the door, grabbing at the steering wheel.

"He has a gun!" Kate cried as Ben got a grip on the driver's wrist and twisted fiercely. But his strength was equaled this time, and for a horrible instant both men held fast, and then the driver swung around wildly, pointing his weapon at Kate and then at Ben, who tightened his grip and pushed upward. The gun fired.

Its deafening report missed them both as it echoed throughout the building. Kate screamed, and the sound of her terror generated an extra rush of adrenaline from Ben, who slammed the man's wrist downward, causing the gun to clatter to the floor.

But the driver continued fighting blindly, powerfully, trying to hurl Ben out of the way. That was when Kate became a dynamo of energy as she scratched and flailed. Between the two of them, Kate pushing and Ben pulling, they forced the driver aside.

In a final move, Ben slammed his fist into Santa's face, hurled him from the car, taking his place in the driver's seat and bringing the car to a full stop.

They'd hit half a dozen other cars in the melee, and as Ben stepped on the brake, the security guard, recovered gun in hand, was beside the car.

"Okay, all of you, both Santas and the woman, hands up!"

Ben and Kate climbed slowly out of the car, and Dylan struggled to his feet. The guard was serious, gun steady in one hand, as he called for backup on his walkie-talkie. "Now what the devil is going on here?" he asked.

Dylan leaned against a pillar, his red suit torn, his face battered. "This man and woman tried to hijack me."

"That's a lie!" Kate broke in. "He tried to kidnap me. There're witnesses, two women. And he's a murderer. He killed my friend, Coral Lampiere."

Dylan attempted a cool look of disbelief. "She's insane. The truth is that she's been stalking me, hanging out where I work, wearing some kind of a disguise. I recognize her now."

The guard shook his head in confusion. "This looks like a situation for the police to straighten out, and they'll be here soon. Everybody just relax and don't try nothing." He cut his eyes at Ben. "Especially you. We got a score to settle."

"Sorry for knocking you down," Ben said, "But I had to get to Kate. This guy was going to kill her—"

"You're nuts," was Dylan's response. Blood was dripping from his nose, and he wiped it away with the sleeve of his jacket.

Kate's fear was replaced by a bright burning anger. It was stronger than the throbbing pain in her head. If they believed him, Dylan could get away with his ridiculous story that she and Ben were the culprits! She had to take a chance. "I saw you that night, Dylan. That's why I came to the spa."

"You see—you see—" he said to the guard. "She's confessing that she came after me!"

"Give it up," Ben said roughly. "We found Coral's body, and we know you did it."

Dylan's face blanched and his eyes roved from Kate to Ben and back again. "You don't know what you're saying."

"You left your cap at the scene, Dylan," Ben persisted.

"No!"

Kate jumped in. "I bet there are fingerprints, too."

"That's where you're wrong." For a moment, Dylan looked almost confident. "She wiped them—I mean—"

"She?" Ben looked over at Kate. Now they both knew—Dylan hadn't acted alone!

Kate felt her pulse race. She remembered how the janitor had bolted and run. He'd been afraid. Now she had to play on that fear. "You didn't do it alone, did you, Dylan? You were too afraid, but someone else was there, someone strong. It was Jennifer's idea, wasn't it?" she chanced.

"No—no—no—" He shook his head hopelessly as if to make her words vanish.

The guard spoke up. "This guy really murdered someone?"

"Yes," Ben said. "He did."

"I didn't," he cried out. "You don't have any proof."

"But we do." Ben's voice was totally convincing. "You can't run and you can't hide, Dylan. We've got too much evidence. The best choice is to make a deal. Otherwise, you're going to jail, and Jennifer is going free."

"No, she wouldn't do that! Would she?"

"You know her better than we do," Kate said. She thought of Jennifer's cold, hard eyes. "But I imagine she'd do just about anything. Even set you up to take the blame."

Dylan looked shattered. "She told me she wiped the prints off Coral's car when we dumped it. She told me it would be okay. It would look like an accident in the spring when the car was found. Everyone would think she'd run off the road. She said no one would know. Jennifer came up with the cruise story, not me."

Tears were cascading down Dylan's swollen face. He was no longer the handsome young trainer from the spa, but a pitiful broken child.

Ben kept pressing. "Why'd Jennifer do it?"

"I figured out the call girl ring, and Jennifer wanted in. So we went to Coral. She said she'd close the operation down before she'd give us a cut. She knew we'd been nosing around and she was already looking for replacements for us. Jennifer and Coral started yelling at each other, and I tried to stop them—" He fell to his knees, shoulders shaking.

"I didn't mean to kill Coral. I just grabbed her neck and—" He looked up at Ben and Kate through bleary eyes. "If Jennifer had come today things would have been different. I told her to come. I said I needed help, but she said Mark would be suspicious with both of us gone. I think he knew about our affair.... Was she setting me up today?"

The wail of a siren intensified as a police car wheeled into the garage. The guard's attention was totally on Dylan. "That's a hell of a story," he said.

Kate felt suddenly dizzy. She swayed a little and reached out for Ben. He took her in his arms. "It's over," he said. "It's really over."

# Chapter Thirteen

"Do you think you'd be more comfortable in bed, Kate?" Joan asked.

Kate shook her head and then winced slightly at the pain caused by the movement. "No, the sofa is fine. The doctor said all I need is twenty-four hours observation."

"We can take care of you here," Joan promised. They were in the living room of the Lakewood house, waiting for Joan's husband to return with the kids and two large pizzas.

"Thanks. I need to be around friends." She gave a shudder, thinking of Dylan's hands on her. Those hands had killed her friend—and could have killed her! "It seems strange," she mused, "to be warm and safe here when only hours ago I was close to death." She turned to Ben, and her eyes showed her gratitude.

"We don't have to talk about it anymore," Ben assured her.

"It helps to talk," Kate replied. "That way, I won't dream about it."

"And I want to hear everything," Joan jumped in. "First you believed someone wanted Kate out of the way to get at the baby, but that wasn't true. Then you decided her life was in danger because of the call girl ring...."

"But it was really because of what she saw," Ben explained. "Kate went to the spa for an appointment, found the place closed and saw a janitor pushing a big trash cart."

"Only the man wasn't a janitor," Kate said. "He was Dylan, one of the spa trainers. I tried to ask him about the spa but he turned and ran. He thought I saw his face, but I didn't."

"That's where the red hair and red coat comes in," Ben explained to his sister. "Kate was too damned easy to identify. He never got a glimpse of her face that night, but he remembered the hair and coat."

"He knew who I was because he'd seen my name on a calendar when he'd been in Coral's office, and he and Jennifer, his lover, decided to get rid of me. Thus the gunshot and the threats. I'm not sure if he really wanted to kill me or just make me go away and forget about Coral. He even tried a break-in at the office—"

"All of this, I imagine, planned by Jennifer," Ben commented.

Kate nodded. "All along I suspected Mark, but he was almost as ignorant as we were at first. He must have known something was going on, though. Remember the day I saw them arguing at the spa?" She spoke carefully, sorting out the information in her mind. "Dylan and Jennifer were having an affair, and he was probably getting wise to them. Now both of them are in jail. And as for the spa—I guess Mark will keep that going for a while."

Joan was wide-eyed. "It's hard to believe that you two were involved in something so frightening."

Kate agreed. "I'm finding *all* this difficult to believe. I still can't accept that Coral is dead, any more than I can believe her involvement in the call girl ring, but the evidence is all there."

"And you and Ben unearthed it," Joan said proudly. "And if that hadn't happened, you wouldn't be together. We wouldn't have Amanda in our family. Now, speaking of family, I hope you'll both be here for Christmas day."

Ben's response was immediate. "Sorry, Sis, I'm on my way to Mexico. You know I love you, but these family gatherings are too much for me." He glanced at Kate as if for affirmation. "Besides, Kate and I both made separate plans for the holidays. We never meant to spend Christmas together, did we?"

Kate tried to meet his eyes evenly as she nodded in faint agreement. "Amanda and I are going to Florida. We'll be with family there."

Joan's face fell. "But I thought...I was sure—" She looked from Kate to Ben, her face registering embarrassment.

Kate stepped in and tried to fill her own empty hurt with a flurry of words that would get Joan off the hook. "Ben and I are great friends, Joan. He's been a wonderful help, taking care of me and Amanda, and of course being my detective partner." She managed a smile. "But I understand that he needs his space."

She'd always hated the phrase and wondered why she'd felt compelled to use it in explaining Ben to his own sister. The whole thing sounded so manufactured and trite. And false. Which of course it was...on her part, anyway.

Ben jumped in, apparently to smooth things over with both women. "I'll be seeing Kate and Mandy when I get back. There's a great friendship among the three of us, and I certainly don't want to give it up. Do you, Kate?''

An awkward silence fell over the room, broken finally by the sound of a car door slamming and the babble of children's voices. "I'll go help with the pizza and the kids." Ben got up quickly and left the room to the women.

THINGS WERE going downhill fast, Kate decided as she hurried to get dinner ready for herself and Amanda. They'd been back in the apartment for three hectic days, and life was not getting any easier. How could any child get used to what Amanda had gone through and was still going through, thanks to Kate's frenetic life-style? Permanence, which kids needed most, hadn't been evident in Amanda's life since her parents died.

And what about what adults needed? It was true that not being shot at or hit over the head was a relief, but in a way Kate missed the excitement of the chase. And she missed Ben. It would be absurd to deny that.

Amanda, tired of playing on the kitchen floor, scooted toward the living room. Kate followed and sank tiredly into a chair as Amanda crossed the room on hands and knees, looking back a couple of times to make sure Kate was watching. Then she pulled herself to a standing position at the coffee table. "Mama."

Kate laughed. She was getting used to the title but it still didn't seem to fit. What exactly was her relationship with this adorable child? She was still considering the problem when Amanda grinned at her, let go of the table and made a wobbly move forward.

Kate saw the grin and smiled back. Only then did she realize what was happening. The baby had taken a step—unassisted. Amanda was walking!

"Amanda!" Kate tried to keep her voice soft and controlled, not showing her excitement as Amanda took a second step, flailed her arms for balance and then toppled backward—and crashed into the table before Kate could get to her.

She swept the screaming child into her arms in one movement and in the next grabbed the telephone and punched in 911.

"Is this an emergency?" a voice asked.

"Yes! Yes! My baby hit her head—"

"I GUESS I OVERREACTED," Kate told Tina the next day. "There was just a little bump on Amanda's head, but she was yelling so loudly I could hardly hear the 911 operator."

"What'd she say?"

"To hang up and call my local pediatrician. She said it wasn't an emergency, and I felt like a fool."

"You aren't a fool," Tina assured her. "You're just a—"

"First-time mother," Kate finished for her. "I know. I've heard the expression every time I've been to Amanda's doctor."

"After a little experience you'll be fine," Tina encouraged. "This kind of thing won't happen again."

"Oh, it'll happen, Tina, at least it would happen if I gave it a chance. But I'm not going to. That's why we're going to Florida. This visit is going to be a test. If it works out, Jack and Laura will legally adopt Amanda."

"You'd let them do that?" Tina was horrified.

"*Let* them?" Kate repeated. "I'll be grateful to them, but more importantly, in the long run, Amanda will be much better off. Look at me, Tina. The baby's recent life has been a mess. First, I got involved in Coral's murder—"

"Inadvertently."

"But it put Amanda in all kinds of danger."

"That won't happen again," Tina replied.

"Then we went to Ben's where she bonded to him and loved him and started to rely on him, and now he's opted out of our lives."

"Rat," Tina murmured.

"No," Kate defended. "He was always up-front and honest. He said he'd had too much family as a kid and wasn't interested in more."

"But you didn't know—"

"'Course I did," Kate denied. "I knew everything when I got involved, and I did it anyway. You know why?" she asked.

Tina hesitated.

"Because I wanted to, Tina. And because he was there when we needed him. That's all anyone can ask."

"Humph," Tina muttered. "I'd ask more."

"What would be the point? He made it clear from the first that commitment wasn't a word in his vocabulary. Why should I be surprised that he's happy to be back to his old life? When he moved us back to my apartment, he talked about staying in touch. He said he'd call us after the holidays, asked me to be sure and invite him to Amanda's birthday party in January, said—"

"The old 'let's be friends routine,'" Tina said darkly.

Kate didn't respond. This was her problem, not Tina's. After a while she admitted, "Now that we're on our own, Amanda and I, it's obvious I'm not much of a mother."

"You found a day-care center," Tina reminded her.

"It's only temporary, but with Laura and Jack, I know she'll be well taken care of and loved. There'll be no guesswork and no insecurity, with two parents at home to see to all her needs."

"But how do they feel? I can't believe they want a kid at their stage of life."

"Obviously, they thought they were finished with child rearing, but they also understand the problem. They're family, and they're willing to help out."

"Willing?" Tina prodded.

"Let's say they're cautiously optimistic," Kate said.

Tina shook her head. "Well, I'm *pessimistic*. This is a big mistake, boss. You and the kid belong together. She loves you."

"And I adore her," Kate admitted, "but I'm trying not to be selfish. I want her to have what I never had, a family of her own." Kate's voice trembled, and she realized she was about to lose control. "I've made up my mind," she said decisively.

Tina nodded. "You're a stubborn woman so I know what that means." Then she asked philosophically, "What can I do to help?"

"Take us to the airport tomorrow. I know it's an imposition, but with all the baby's gear I can't do this alone."

"Don't worry. I'll be there."

Kate checked her watch and reached for her coat. "I have an appointment with United Charities at two and then . . ."

Tina waved her out the door. "I'll take care of things here. Get going and good luck."

The moment she heard the elevator doors open and then close on Kate, Tina reached for the phone, pulled a number from her Rolodex and dialed.

"Pick up," she mouthed to herself. "Be there."

She let out a long sigh of relief when she heard the click of the receiver at the other end.

"This is Tina at ESS. I need to talk with you—"

"THIS IS RIGHT. This is for the best." Kate talked out loud as she flung clothes into her suitcase. "Laura and Jack can give Amanda everything I can't. It doesn't matter how I feel because..." She began to repeat the litany again. "This is right. This is for the best...."

She finished packing, wiped her tears away and zipped Amanda into her snowsuit. When Amanda smiled up at her, Kate felt the sting of tears and almost lost control of her emotions again.

Then she heard the knock on her apartment door. Tina was early. "Coming," she called. She took a quick glance in the mirror, satisfied that she didn't look as if she'd been blubbering half the day. With Amanda in her arms, she went down the hall and opened the door—but not to Tina.

"Hello," Ben said with an easy smile. "Heard you needed a ride to the airport."

"Ben..." Kate took a moment to recover. He looked wonderful, tall and handsome, with a feathering of snow dusting his black leather jacket and gleaming in his hair. She felt the familiar rush of excitement at seeing him. As usual, his presence dominated the space around them.

"I thought Tina was—"

"She was," Ben said. "But something came up so she called me to step in. As it turns out, we're leaving for our vacations at just about the same time. So why not drive to the airport together?"

He held out his arms to Amanda, and Kate released the squirming baby to him.

"Hi, Mandy. How ya been?" Round, blue eyes shining, she gurgled delightedly. "And how are you doing, Kate?"

"All right." She forced a smile.

"So you've decided to take Mandy to your cousins for good?"

"Tina told you," she said with a sigh.

"And about Mandy's fall, too." He checked the baby out, tenderly touching the small bump on her head, smoothing back her golden curls. "She seems fine. Don't be hard on yourself. All kids have accidents. There'll be more. Bruises, broken limbs, even teeth knocked out. It comes with the territory."

"But I don't know how to handle the territory. That's the problem." Her voice was sharper than she meant it to be.

"You're taking her to Florida because of one little fall?"

Kate looked away. "Plus everything else that's happened. I was on the phone with Laura and Jack for hours. We've discussed everything, and I think this is the best solution for Amanda."

"For God's sake, why?" he asked angrily.

"You know why," she burst out, "better than anyone. You know firsthand what an inadequate mother I am. Amanda needs so much that I can't give her." She struggled for control. "I've made the decision."

"I don't think it's a good one, Kate," he said as he tried to stay calm.

Her eyes met his coolly. "But it's mine, isn't it? I'm the one with all the responsibility so I make the choices."

His mouth tightened. "You're right. I was out of line. This had nothing to do with me." He walked purposefully toward the bedroom, where he picked up Kate's bag. "Let's get going."

IT SEEMED so familiar, Kate thought, riding in Ben's car with Amanda dozing in her car seat. Except today, they weren't talking. His handsome profile seemed carved in stone.

He finally broke the silence. "Traffic's building up already. The airport will be a madhouse." He tapped the brakes, slowed the car to a crawl and turned to her. "Listen, Kate, I know this is none of my business, but I still have to tell you what I think."

She remained silent.

"You should reconsider this Florida deal. So you don't know everything about raising a child, but... love is what counts. You love Amanda, and she loves you."

"Amanda's very adaptable," Kate said. "She'll bond with Laura and Jack." She paused before adding adamantly, "She's too wonderful a baby not to have the best—two reliable, experienced parents who love her."

The traffic began to move, and he eased down on the accelerator. "And you're too stubborn to see what's right in front of you. You and Mandy are a family. Why are you fighting that?"

She thought before answering. "Maybe because I'm scared."

"You? Come on. You broke into the spa, outran a security guard, fought off Dylan. You're not afraid of anything, Kate."

"Of course, I am. We're all afraid of something, and my fear is I'll fail with Amanda. I couldn't bear to hurt her."

"I never thought you'd run away from anything, Kate."

"I guess we all run at some time," she said softly. "Even you."

BEN, BUCKLED in his seat on the aircraft, shut his eyes and tried to think of the trip ahead, but all he could see was Kate, the unreadable look in her eyes when he said goodbye at her gate, her smile, Mandy's tears.

Why did their faces keep invading his mind and heart? He had everything he wanted. A great life. Freedom. Money. Time. But somehow all that didn't seem enough.

The pilot's voice came over the intercom. "Sorry for the delay, folks, but we're faced with holiday traffic and holiday weather. We'll be taxiing away from the gate in approximately ten minutes. So sit back and relax."

AT HER GATE, Kate stood patiently at the head of the check-in line where the agent checked her boarding pass.

"Just a slight delay, Ms. McNair. We'll be boarding shortly, and I'll call for passengers with children first."

Kate nodded, shifted Amanda in her arms and sat back down. Amanda seemed fascinated by the lights and sounds of the airport and sat quietly in Kate's lap. Now and then she'd see a tall dark-haired man and point, asking "Da-da?"

"No, darling. I'm afraid not."

Kate looked at the clock above the desk. Assuming Ben's flight was on schedule, he'd already taken off and was on his way to Mexico and his old life. She couldn't help feeling anger at Tina for arranging their encounter, even though she knew her assistant meant well.

But seeing Ben had only made the hurt in her heart more intense. He didn't love her; that was obvious. Sure, he cared about her and Amanda, but only as a fleeting part of his life.

Why had she ever thought it would be different?

Because she loved him!

"Ma-ma." Amanda looked up and smiled, and that trusting, loving expression tugged at her heart. The baby had total faith in her. Tears stung Kate's eyes. She didn't deserve that trust!

To her surprise, Amanda turned away from the fascinating crowd of travelers, put her pudgy arms around Kate's neck and clung lovingly. Then she leaned back and touched Kate's wet cheeks. What was going on with this enchanting baby? Was Amanda trying to sway her and change her mind?

Of course not! She was simply reacting instinctively. But what loving instincts!

"Ma-ma," Amanda repeated as she leaned forward and planted a wet kiss on her cheek.

Tina's voice invaded Kate's mind. *She loves you, Kate.*

Ben's voice joined in, speaking words he'd said only half an hour ago. *You and Mandy are a family.*

Kate tightened her arms around the baby and felt the cold hard pain she'd been carrying inside suddenly melt and fill her with a surge of warmth. All the planning, the phone calls to Jack and Laura, her rationalizations, came down to this: a baby in her arms, blue eyes shining with love and trust.

Her flight was called, and Kate stood up, holding Amanda tightly. Yes, they would spend Christmas with Laura and Jack. After that, she could only hope that her cousins would understand her decision.

"Here we go, babe. Time to fly."

"I'M SORRY, SIR, but we're ready to close the exit door." The attendant on Ben's flight was polite but firm.

"I suggest you change your mind," Ben offered, "because I'm getting off this plane now."

"Is there an emergency, sir?" A male officer materialized from the flight deck.

"You could say that," Ben told him. "The woman I love is about to make the biggest mistake of her life." Ben realized that he was smiling. *The woman I love.* Dammit, that sounded good. "The crew hasn't prepared for takeoff yet so will you please let me deplane?"

The attendant stepped aside, and Ben bolted through the boarding ramp. Kate's gate was at the other end of the huge terminal, and he sprinted toward it, not stopping to look at the departure screen, just hoping that she'd also been delayed. He elbowed past the throngs of travelers, dodging, pushing people aside, not caring about the dirty looks or threatening comments.

Then he saw her gate up ahead. The plane was still on the ground! He caught a glimpse of Kate's red hair. The agent was taking her ticket, and Amanda was waving goodbye.

"Stop that woman!" he cried. "She has my baby!"

Kate whirled and looked wildly around in time to see Ben jumping over a row of chairs as if it were an Olympic high hurdle. He called out to them, "Don't get on that plane!"

"Da-da!" Amanda cried.

Ben was beside them, pulling Kate out of line and into his arms. "Stay with me, please, Kate." There was urgency in his face and voice.

"I thought you were on the way to Mexico," she stammered. "I thought—"

"Why would I go away when everything I want is right here? I love you, Kate. I want to marry you—and Mandy!" He kissed her long and hard, and only when the crowd around them began to applaud did he end the kiss.

"I love you, too," she murmured, "but loving is a commitment, and you said—"

"Whatever I said, I was wrong." He rescued Amanda, who had been squeezed between them, and hoisted her into the air. "Merry Christmas, Mandy. What do you say we go shopping for a tree and presents and stockings?"

He took Kate's arm and pulled her out of the flow of the crowd. "You're the right mother for Mandy. And I'm the right father. We can handle it, Kate. Together. Get on a phone, call your cousins and say Mandy stays with you."

Kate burst into laughter. "I'd already decided to tell them that! I couldn't get along without my baby, any more than I can get along without you." He kissed her again, oblivious to the hurrying passengers all around them. "Merry Christmas, Kate."

"Merry Christmas, darling."

Amanda, secure in Ben's arms, reached out a small hand toward each of them. "Ma-ma, Da-da."

Ben and Kate looked at each other and laughed.

"This time, you're exactly right, Mandy," he said. "Come on, let's go home."

## HARLEQUIN®

# I N T R I G U E®

In steamy New Orleans, three women witnessed the same crime, testified against the same man and were then swept into the Witness Protection Program. But now, there's new evidence. These three women are about to come out of hiding—and find both danger and desire....

# eye WITNESS

Start your new year right with all the books in the exciting EYEWITNESS miniseries:

Don't miss these three books—or miss out on all the passion and drama of the crime of the century!

Look us up on-line at: http://www.romance.net

EYE1

# HARLEQUIN ®

## Scandals

A passionate story of romance, where bold, daring characters
set out to defy their world of propriety and strict social codes.

*"Scandals*—a story that will make your heart race and your
pulse pound. Spectacular!"                        —Suzanne Forster

"Devon is daring, dangerous and altogether delicious."
                                                        —Amanda Quick

Don't miss this wonderful full-length novel from Regency
favorite Georgina Devon.

Available in December, wherever Harlequin books are sold.

# The collection of the year!
## *NEW YORK TIMES* BESTSELLING AUTHORS

**Linda Lael Miller**
*Wild About Harry*

**Janet Dailey**
*Sweet Promise*

**Elizabeth Lowell**
*Reckless Love*

**Penny Jordan**
*Love's Choices*

and featuring
**Nora Roberts**
*The Calhoun Women*

This special trade-size edition features four of the wildly
popular titles in the Calhoun miniseries together in
one volume—a true collector's item!

Pick up these great authors and a chance to win
a weekend for two in New York City at the
Marriott Marquis Hotel on Broadway! We'll pay
for your flight, your hotel—even a Broadway show!

Available in December at your favorite retail outlet.

**NEW YORK**
**Marriott.®**
**MARQUIS**

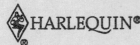 

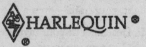

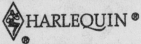

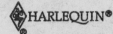

# 1997

## Reader's Engagement Book
## A calendar of important dates
## and anniversaries for readers to use!

Informative and entertaining—with notable
dates and trivia highlighted throughout the year.

Handy, convenient, pocketbook size to help you
keep track of your own personal important dates.

Added bonus—contains $5.00 worth of coupons
for upcoming Harlequin and Silhouette books.
This calendar more than pays for itself!

 Available beginning in November at
your favorite retail outlet.

*Weddings by DeWilde*

Since the turn of the century the elegant and fashionable
DeWilde stores have helped brides around the world
turn the fantasy of their "Special Day" into reality. But now the
store and three generations of family are torn apart by the
separation of Grace and Jeffrey DeWilde. Family members
face new challenges and loves in this fast-paced, glamorous,
internationally set series. For weddings and romance, glamour
and fun-filled entertainment, enter the world of DeWildes....

## Watch for *WILDE MAN*,
### by Daphne Clair
### Coming to you in January, 1997

The sophisticated image and spotless reputation of DeWilde's
Sydney store was being destroyed by tacky T-shirts and
unmentionable souvenirs! And Maxine Sterling was not going
to let swaggering DeWilde Cutter get away with it! He'd have
to take his gorgeous looks and puzzling name and find
another business. And she was certainly *not* going to fall in
love with a man whose life-style symbolized everything
she'd fought so hard to escape!

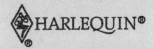

HARLEQUIN®